# the MONSTER DOCTOR

## JOHN KELLY

## REVOLTING RESCUE

First published 2020 by Macmillan Children's Books
an imprint of Pan Macmillan
The Smithson, 6 Briset Street, London EC1M 5NR
Associated companies throughout the world
www.panmacmillan.com

ISBN 978-1-5290-2133-2

135798642

A CIP catalogue record for this book is available
from the British Library.

Printed and bound by CPI Group (UK) Ltd, Croydon CR0 4YY

MIX
Paper from
responsible sources
FSC® C116313
FSC
www.fsc.org

To the real doctors out there who
looked after everyone while I sat at
home drawing all these silly pictures.

# CONTENTS:

# A DOG AT EACH END

## Chapter 1

I was heading down the street towards the monster doctor's surgery when I saw Morty the zombie walking a **zombie dog**. I'd just rounded that corner where the human world turns into the monster world. You might know the place? It's just past the unicycle repair shop, but before **VLAD THE VAMPIRE'S** all-night garage and convenience store.

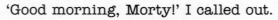

'Good morning, Morty!' I called out.

'Morning, Ozzy!' wheezed Morty.

To my surprise, he looked quite smart. Most of his limbs were intact, and his **eyeballs** and **ears** were all where they were supposed to be. Even his head had stayed where I'd glued it back on last week, and **amazingly** nothing else had fallen off in the meantime.

His dog, on the other hand, was a scruffy black-and-white thing.

'What's his name?' I asked.

'Tug,' Morty replied.

Tug grinned up at me with a mouth as **gappy as Stonehenge.** He seemed happy enough, considering he was a zombie dog, but I noticed that his nose was missing.

'Your dog's got no nose!' I said.

Morty grinned. 'That depends on which end you're looking at.'

The other end of the dog – the end where it's traditional to have a **bottom** – had a completely different dog's head. Unlike Tug, this one looked pretty good. He had short black hair, a mouth full of teeth and a nice shiny nose.

'Isn't it a problem that your dog – or dogs – have no bottom between them?' I asked.

'Not really,' Morty said. 'It actually saves me *a small fortune in poo bags.* Which isn't to be sniffed at.'

(Unless you were a zombie dog with no nose, of course.)

'What's this one's name?'

'She's called War!' Morty sniggered. **'Tug! War!** Geddit?' And he laughed until both his **ears** dropped off.

I picked them up and popped them in my pocket.

'Come on, Morty,' I said. 'I'll walk you to the surgery and stitch these back on for you.'

'Speak up, Ozzy!' he said. 'I seem to suddenly have gone a bit deaf!'

So I asked him again in a louder voice.

'That's very kind,' he said. 'But I was heading there anyway. War's been a bit poorly since she **ate two postman's legs last week!'** I wasn't sure whether the legs were from more than one postman. And I forgot to ask later – what with everything that happened.

We had just crossed the road by **The Battered Squid** chippy and passed beneath the new street sign that stated:

## NO SPONTANEOUS COMBUSTION BETWEEN 11 P.M. & 7 A.M.

when a question occurred to me.

'Shouldn't you take Tug-o-War to a monster vet?' I asked. But he just shook his head and pointed to the logo on my **MONSTER DOCTOR TRAINEE** T-shirt.

It said 'CURA OMNIA', which is Latin for **HEAL ANYTHING** and is the motto of the **Monster Doctors' Organisation.**

Morty was right, of course. The distinction between monsters and things* and their pets is a bit pointless when either one of them might have two hundred and seven tentacles.

\* Monsters and things are very different.

Monsters are born weird.

Things are made weird by events.

All 'thing' types are classified by a simple letter code. For example, Morty is a 'D-T' which stands for Dead Thing.

For more about monsters and things see Ogbert & Nish's *Monster Maladies* or the more definitive reference book *10,001 Interesting Things About Things*.

We rounded the corner into Lovecraft Avenue and there, dead ahead, was the **monster doctor's surgery.**

It stands (or rather leans) somewhere between five and seven storeys high. When I'd first seen it at the beginning of the school holidays, **large bits** of it had been regularly falling off. This was due to both the doctor's funding issues (i.e. total lack of) and a nasty leak from the **third-storey swamp-creature treatment suite.**

But after the doctor and I had cured the life-threatening indigestion of an enormous **DRAGON** called Carol, which had involved her swallowing me and then **explosively vomiting** me out between her razor-sharp jaws, she had given us a great big bag of gold coins as a thank-you. So the doctor could now afford the urgent repairs.

Morty and I paused before the surgery's now familiar brass plaque.

10 *Lovecraft Avenue*
## *Annie von Sichertall* VIII
### M.D.F.R.S.C.D.
**Fully qualified monster physician & surgeon**
**Anything treated**
(*No biting allowed within these premises*)

'C'mon, Morty,' I said.

I was looking forward to the nice simple job of **stitching a zombie's ears back on**, and was just thinking of the cup of tea and biscuit I'd have afterwards, when the most **awful** noise erupted from inside the surgery.

# STAMPEDE

## Chapter 2

This wasn't the normal everyday cacophony of the monster doctor's surgery. That was usually just patients moaning about their **ingrowing eyeballs,** their **leaky brains** and how **rude** Delores (our grumpy receptionist) had been to them (i.e. very).

This was a noise I'd **never** heard before. Neither had Morty.

'What on earth is that dreadful banging?' He winced.

'Well,' I mused, 'it sounds a lot like someone hammering nails in with a saucepan while being slapped very hard with a large, wet bath towel.' But, as **weird** as things can get at the surgery, I was almost entirely certain it wasn't that.

The **banging** got even louder.

'Perhaps Delores caught the doctor trying to get into her special biscuit tin again,' said Morty. 'And she hit her with the—'

But his interesting theory was cut off by shrieks of terror as the surgery's front doors **crashed** open.

Morty and I jumped out of the way as a stampede of patients ran, slithered, crawled, hopped, limped and flew away from the surgery in every possible direction.

'BY MY SLIGHTLY SAGGY STITCHING!' cried Morty, backing nervously away. 'They look as panicked as if they've seen a *cutie!*'

'A what?' I asked. But Morty wasn't listening – either that or he couldn't hear me (his ears had fallen off earlier, remember).

Tug and War were whining noisily and straining at their lead to get away.

'Surely it can't be a *cutie* – can it?' Morty muttered as he continued retreating.

'My friend Astrogoth saw one and **three of his eyeballs—**' But the fate of Astrogoth's eyeballs was cut short by an agitated scream from the doorway.

'That **HORRIBLE** thing is right BEHIND US!' wailed a many-tentacled patient called Mrs Fingerling. She was trying to get past Mr Ooozull,

a **snail monster,** who was stuck in the doorway.
'GET OUT OF MY WAY, you **flobbering**
SLOWCOACH!' she cried, while frantically
scrabbling at his giant shell with her mass of
tentacles. She was staring wide-eyed with terror
back into the surgery. 'IT'S GOING TO
EAT EVERYONE!'

'I'm . . . moving . . . as . . . fast . . . as . . .
I . . .' said Mr Ooozull as he finally managed
to **squeeze** out of the door. Mrs Fingerling
**sqweeched** with relief and **flolloped** off down
the street. In seconds, there were no monster
patients anywhere near the surgery. Apart from
Mr Ooozull, of course, who was just finishing his
sentence.

'. . . can, Muriel!'

The crazy banging and slapping from inside
the surgery had grown even louder. Morty's dogs
were still straining frantically at their lead to get
away, and Morty wasn't much calmer. His eyes
were wide with fear.

'What on earth are you three so afraid of?' I
asked. 'Surely there's nothing that can hurt you.
**You're dead!'**

'You ordinaries!' Morty scoffed. 'You have no idea how **dangerous** a cutie is to monsters and things! And just because zombies are dead doesn't mean they haven't still got a lot to live for!' And with that Tug yanked on his lead so hard that **Morty's entire left arm came off**. Tug (and War) bounded off down Lovecraft Avenue, trailing the lead – and Morty's arm – behind them.

'WAIT FOR ME, you little . . .!' yelled Morty as he chased after them at the fastest pace his stitches would allow – without too many other body parts dropping off!

'WHAT'S A CUTIE?' I shouted after him, but he didn't hear me. (Which may have been on account of both his ears falling off earlier, I suppose.)

**This was really odd!** How could something called a cutie be so scary to all these monsters – even a zombie? Cutie certainly didn't sound scary. In fact it sounded quite nice.

**I was intrigued.**

I had to get inside and find out what was going on.

But I had barely taken a step when something that looked a lot like a **cannonball,** only much larger and made out of tweed,* exploded out of one of the surgery's downstairs windows.

* They don't make cannonballs out of tweed, by the way. I checked at wwmw.custom-cannonballs. com. Although if you are interested they are available in iron, concrete, steel and even bright yellow hi-vis rubber (for safety battles).

# VEG

## Chapter 3

As a **trainee monster doctor** you get used to surprises. (Things like being **vomited** out of a giant **DRAGON** certainly help, I suppose.) But a cannonball blasting out of a downstairs window, bouncing off the pavement and saying, quite clearly, **'OW!'** still took me aback.

It rolled to a stop right at my feet and one side of it **magically** sprouted a thick arm, followed moments later by an identical one on the opposite side. When a pair of scrawny legs clad in *thick woollen tights* popped out, I realized that this wasn't a cannonball at all.

**It was the monster doctor.**

She frowned up at me through her tinted glasses. 'Ah!' she said. 'Nurse Ordinary.

How **SUPER** of you to finally show up for work.' She clambered to her knees and began to tidy her hair (a daunting task at the best of times). 'If you're not too busy **Insta-Twitt-Booking your belly fluff** – or whatever it is you young folk do since they banned **mammoth racing** – I would appreciate a hand with some **actual real-life monster medicine.** I have an instructive case for you inside.'

'Is it a cutie?' I asked, pointing down at the green *tendril* that was busy *twining* itself round the doctor's left ankle. The doctor fixed me with the expression she uses when I have just said something that she considers **extremely stupid.**

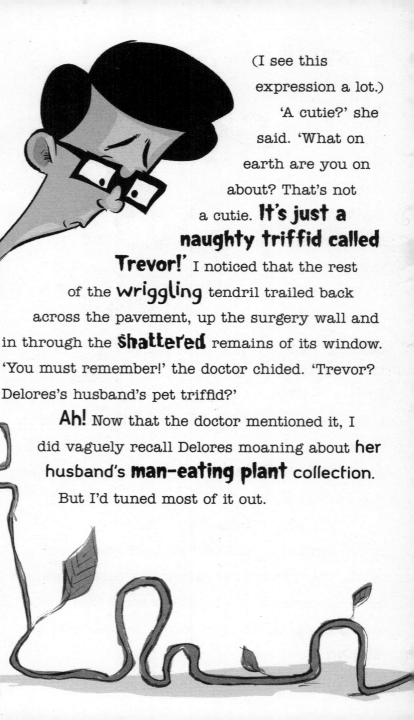

(I see this expression a lot.) 'A cutie?' she said. 'What on earth are you on about? That's not a cutie. **It's just a naughty triffid called Trevor!'** I noticed that the rest of the **wriggling** tendril trailed back across the pavement, up the surgery wall and in through the **shattered** remains of its window. 'You must remember!' the doctor chided. 'Trevor? Delores's husband's pet triffid?'

**Ah!** Now that the doctor mentioned it, I did vaguely recall Delores moaning about **her** husband's **man-eating plant** collection. But I'd tuned most of it out.

(That's not rude by the way. The doctor warned me in my first week that listening to Delores moan for more than five minutes is as dangerous to your health as eating a **Black plague and raspberry yogurt.**)

'Is Trevor the one that's always trying to eat Delores when she's asleep?' I asked.

'Yes,' said the doctor. 'Which is, of course, *perfectly* normal behaviour for an under-watered triffid.' But, as she spoke, the adventurous tendril began tugging very firmly on the doctor's sturdy left thigh. She smacked it hard with her hand. **'Naughty Trevor! Bad triffid!'** The triffid recoiled briefly, but then it gained courage and tightened its grip on her leg again. 'Oh dear,' she said. 'This is worse than I thought.' And there was suddenly more urgency in her voice as she asked, 'Have you brought your copy of OGBERT AND NISH'S MONSTER MALADIES with you today?'

'**Absolutely!**' I said, rummaging around in my satchel for the essential (and highly portable) reference book. 'I was reading it in bed only last night. The section on **Diseases of Teachers** is completely fascinating. I never knew they had to eat a cupful of **spiders** every day or they'll turn into—'

But, before I could finish, Trevor's tendril twined round the doctor's waist like a **vegetable lasso** and she was yanked violently away.

As Trevor pulled her roughly up the wall, she yelled, 'Ozzy! **Get me a fresh SPONGE WORM from the pharm—**'

But she was cut off as the **horrid** plant pulled her roughly back in through the surgery's broken window. I hastily opened my trusty copy of **OGBERT AND NISH** and turned to the section on triffids. I began to read very, **VERY** quickly.

# TRIFFIDS

Triffids make excellent pets – despite the popular prejudice against them for eating people. In fact, this very feature can be extremely useful if you have a severe rodent infestation, burglars or just very annoying neighbours who call round without being invited.

There are two common minor ailments of triffids:

## 1. UNDER-WATERING

This will cause the triffid to become very thirsty and shuffle off in search of a drink.

**THIS IS TO BE AVOIDED!**

Triffids should therefore ALWAYS be kept in a pot or container small enough to prevent them from growing walking roots.

## TREATMENT:

ALWAYS MAKE SURE TO OVER-WATER.

274

## 2. Over-watering

This will cause the triffid to grow rapidly and become excessively violent.

## THIS IS TO BE AVOIDED!

### Treatment:

Rapid removal of water. This is a relatively simple process and can be done using a large mining pump or prompt application of Saharan sponge worms.

### WARNING!

This can be complicated by the triffid tearing your limbs off.

275

There is only one major disease of triffids:

## HOMICIDAL RAGE

Triffids must not – under any circumstances – be exposed to flashing infra-violet lights. These can cause a state of homicidal rage in which the triffid will attempt to destroy all intelligent life on earth with a TRIFFID SEED BOMB.

## THIS IS SERIOUSLY TO BE AVOIDED!

So triffids must be kept away from strange comets passing close to the earth, mobile discos and monster emergency vehicles.

### TREATMENT:

The only cure is the precise application of small nuclear weapons. These are not usually available from chemists without a prescription.

**EDITOR'S NOTE:** Triffids have no natural predators. So why they haven't taken over the world yet is a mystery. If you find out, please let myself or Madame Nish know immediately.

*Dr Odichanga Ogbert*

So the good news was that this was a simple case of over-watering. Trevor wasn't about to **destroy all life on earth.**

All I had to do was:

1. Find a sponge worm (whatever that was).

2. Use it to cure an over-watered triffid (however you did that).

3. Try not to get any of my **arms** or **legs** pulled off by a **giant man-eating plant.**

That all seemed pretty straightforward and **dangerously weird** – in the usual monster doctor-ish way. Presumably I'd find the sponge worm in the pharmacy – a small cupboard-sized room just off reception. The doctor had previously told me to stay out of there because apparently some of the monster medicines were **'dangerous to eat'**. Or **'might try to eat you'**. I forget which.

But there wasn't time to worry about that sort of thing. **The doctor was in trouble!** So I flung open the door, charged down the surgery hallway and round the corner into the waiting room where I came face to face with . . .

**Trevor the triffid.**

# TREVOR

## Chapter 4

Trevor was absolutely **ENORMOUS!**
He filled the waiting room about
as completely as an elephant in
a budget airline seat!

The monster doctor was
engaged in what looked like
a combination of **extreme-
gardening** and **MEDIEVAL
COMBAT.** She was using a
battered floral-pattern tea tray as a
shield against Trevor's flailing green
tendrils, while her other hand was
busy with the small **axe** she uses as a
paperweight. The waiting-room floor was
**slick** and shiny with slimy green plant sap.

Delores had barricaded herself inside her receptionist booth and was offering a non-stop stream of complaints.

"'Just give him a bit of water, Delores!" you said. "He's probably feeling a bit peaky, Delores!" you said. It's hardly my fault if I don't know exactly how much water to—'

'PLEASE STOP SPEAKING, DELORES!' bellowed the doctor, as she chopped a tendril off with a very impressive **backhand** stroke. Then she noticed me, parried a sneaky blow from Trevor with the tray and said, 'Ah, Nurse Ordinary! Do you think you might fetch the sponge worm we discussed earlier – while I still have all my limbs?'

I nodded and started towards the pharmacy, but immediately slipped on the sap-slicked floor and fell backwards on to my bottom. This was **extremely** painful, but luckily it meant that a large tendril that had been about to throttle me sailed above my head instead.

As I tried to stand up, a different tendril **thwacked** me hard on the back and I slid across the room towards the open pharmacy door. I hit the wall inside so hard that the door banged shut safely behind me.

I looked up.

**Oh dear.**

Every inch of the wall appeared to be filled with shelves. And those shelves were **crammed** with packets, boxes and bottles of **weird monster medicines** in every size and shape.

bellowed the doctor helpfully from next door. I got to my feet and there, on the left-hand wall (seventh shelf down) I found the extensive 'WORM' section.

**'WHAT IS TAKING YOU SO LONG?'** yelled the doctor between loud **THWACKKS!** on the tray. 'There are only two hundred and seventeen worm-based medicines, for goodness' sake! The sponge worms are just BEHIND the bottle of PLACEBO POISON!'

'**AHA!**' I cried, spotting the large bottle marked with a skull and crossed-tentacles. Behind it was a tiny cardboard packet labelled:

1 SPONGEWORM

Slitheringtons

*Useful for triffid-calming, mopping up flooding or any other embarrassing amounts of moisture.*

## GUARANTEED TO WORK INSTANTLY.

[To ACTIVATE, place near liquid. For larger spillages seek medical attention, the fire brigade or a sturdier brand of underwear.]

I tore the packet open and shook the contents out into my palm.

The sponge worm was an **unimpressive, shrunken little squiggle** that looked like an uninflated yellow **party balloon.** Still, my cute (but horrendous) baby sister has taught me that appearances can be deceptive. So I closed my fingers around the little worm, *flung* open the pharmacy door and sprang into action.

I didn't get very far.

Trevor was waiting. He wrenched the battered tray from the doctor's hands and spun it at me like a *floral-patterned* **Frisbee.** It hit me in the stomach and I doubled over.

## 'OOOOFFFF!'

My hand opened and I watched helplessly as the precious sponge worm flew out of it and across the room.

It was going to miss Trevor completely.

# A CUTIE CALL?

## Chapter 5

L uckily, the doctor had noticed.
**Quick as a flash** she sent the little axe
spinning across the room. The blade struck the
sponge worm a delicate glancing
blow, redirecting
it into a nearby
leaflet carousel.

PLEASE DO **NOT** EAT THE LEAFLETS thank you

LIFESTYLE ADVICE

WHY THAT WAS A REALLY BAD IDEA

NEW & OLD WARNING

The worm bounced off a leaflet warning monsters that **'EATING ROAD SIGNS CAUSES SEVERE FLATULENCE AND IS NOW ILLEGAL!'** and dropped right into Trevor's pot.

There was a really loud **SSSCHLLOOOOOOOOOOOOOOOOOOOOOOOP!** noise – a bit like when you can't get the last bit of milkshake out of the glass – and then Trevor just shrank. One second he was flapping about like a waiter trying to serve **spaghetti in a hurricane,** the next he was as neat and tidy as *Grandma's* ⁊ *shopping-list collection.*

The sponge worm, on the other hand, was now **HUGE.** It lay in Trevor's pot looking very content. Unlike me, who was winded, dazed and wearing trousers soaked in **triffid sap.**

'**WELL PLAYED, Orderly Ozzy!**' The doctor laughed. '**Monster medics – 1. Naughty triffid – 0!**'

She was sitting on the surgery floor brushing leaves out of her haystack of hair. 'That was a bracing way to begin morning surgery! But I suppose we must get on. **DELORES!** Kindly show the next patient in, please.'

'There aren't any patients,' announced Delores, who had emerged from the reception booth once she'd seen it was safe. 'They've all run away. Grown monsters scared of a naughty triffid tantrum!' she said with clear disgust.

'Very well,' said the doctor as she shook thick green sap out of her favourite mug. 'I shall indulge myself with a nice cup of bilge tea and a **chocolate-coated starfish.**' She headed for the kitchen. 'And will someone **PLEASE** answer that phone?'

I had heard the ringing, but thought it was just an after-effect of Trevor **banging** so loudly on the tea tray. I picked up the phone. **'Monster doctor's surgery,'** I said in my poshest telephone voice. 'Orderly Ozzy speaking. How can I help you?'

It was extremely hard to hear the person, thing or monster on the other end of the line, as there was a **siren** going off and a fair bit of shouting in the background. On top of that the speaker was, for some reason, whispering.

'Ah! At last,' murmured the caller. 'I thought you'd never answer!'

'We have been rather bus—' I began, but the speaker cut me off.

'I need to talk to the **monster doctor,**' they breathed down the phone.

'If you could just wait one moment,' I said. 'Who shall I say is calli—?' But I was interrupted again.

'There's no time!' they hissed. 'Just listen! This is VERY important. Tell the MD to get over to Cringetown high street immediately.' The voice dropped to an even more conspiratorial whisper. 'Tell her there's been a major cutie incident in the FANG-TASTIQUE FUN shop. If she hurries, she can get there before that floppy-faced idiot Inspector Pincher does something stupid again.'

They hung up.

'Who was that?' asked the doctor. She was fiddling with the lock on top of the office biscuit tin.

'That was odd,' I said. 'Someone calling to tip you off about a "cutie" incident. Which is weird because that's the third or fourth time today someone has mentioned a cutie. What are they?'

The doctor put the biscuit tin down. Her face had turned **bright green** with shock.*

'Where?' she asked.

'Somewhere called Cringetown,' I replied.

* She's a monster, remember. She doesn't go white with shock. She goes lime-green. She can turn white, but that means she's embarrassed. She also turns yellow when she's happy and a peculiar shade of lilac when she needs the toilet urgently.

'It's OK, though. Someone called Inspector Pincher is already on his way there to deal with it.' But this news didn't seem to reassure her. Instead, she shot up out of her chair as if a **zombie-weasel** had nipped her ankle.

She **bounced** across the waiting room towards the ambulance pole, pausing only to grab her **armour-plated** tweed overcoat, *a packet of chocolate-coated starfish* and **a travel pack of dynamite**. She called over her shoulder, 'Meet me outside in three minutes!' Then she leaped for the green-and-yellow pole that leads down to the basement garage and dropped out of view.

I was left there wondering once more: **What on earth is a cutie?**

I had three minutes. That was more than enough time to sponge the worst of the triffid sap off my trousers while reading what **OGBERT & NISH** had to say about cuties.

# Q-T

## WHAT ARE Q-Ts?

No one knows.

'Q-T' therefore stands for Questionable Thing. (Known by the more common nickname 'cutie'.)

Q-Ts have huge eyes, tiny noses and squeaky high-pitched voices that can cause permanent loss of hearing in more sensitive monsters. Most Q-Ts are covered in a disgustingly soft, fur-like material that only ever seems to come in pastel shades of pink, blue, green or yellow. These colours are deeply unnatural and will cause melting eyeballs in most monsters or things not wearing proper eye protection.

Any physical contact with Q-T entities is DANGEROUS for all monsters and things. It is to be avoided at all costs! Loss of antennae, mandibles, tails, fins, limbs, tentacles, tongues and horns is not unknown. Prolonged contact can lead to DEATH (level 3) – even in zombies.

111

## !!!WARNING!!!

IF YOU BELIEVE THAT YOU MAY HAVE COME IN CONTACT WITH A Q-T, YOU SHOULD CALL THE Q-T CON-MAN TEAM (Q-T CONTAINMENT AND MANAGEMENT TEAM) IMMEDIATELY ON ITS QUICK-DIAL HOTLINE NUMBER:
914-15168327-65-874635-8840-7876-5-1.

## !!!WARNING!!!

# GETTING HAIRY

## Chapter 6

Three minutes later, I was waiting outside
the surgery, trying to shake off the mental
image of my eyeballs melting. I could see
now why these cuties were so **terrifying**
to monsters and things. But there was also
something odd about their physical description.
It reminded me of **something very familiar**.
But I just couldn't think where from.

I was still wondering about it when
Lance roared up in a cloud of leaky
exhaust smoke and drove
all thoughts from
my brain.

I hopped into
the passenger seat.

'**Buckle up!**' said the doctor from the top of her huge pile of driving cushions. (She needed them to reach the steering wheel.) I'd barely got my seat belt fastened before we were *roaring* off down Lovecraft Avenue. Just before we **crashed** through the front window of number 24, where Gordon the ghoul lived, the doctor pulled back Lance's steering wheel and we '**fell off**' our dimension. Which is completely normal when you travel by monster ambulance and is nothing to worry about at all. Honestly.

But I should explain who Lance is.

Lance is the monster doctor's ambulance.

He's as alive as you or I – in some **weird** way

that has never been adequately explained to

me – and can travel anywhere in the six approved

dimensions at will. Which, as you can imagine,

is **terrifically** useful in an emergency.

As we slipped out of
# Dimension 3.14159263 (AHA: the Real World)
the doctor told Bruce* our destination.

* Bruce is Lance's BAT-NAV. All monster ambulances need a BAT-NAV to help them navigate. This is because they have a terrible sense of direction. Bruce lives in the basement with Lance. He spends his time hanging upside down in the dark, playing computer games and listening to thrash metal at very high frequencies.

(Bruce doesn't like me. It's nothing personal, though. He doesn't like anyone, apart from Lance.)

'Cringetown high street!' she snapped. 'And no scenic detours across the Great Barrier Reef today, if you please. This is an **EMERGENCY!'**

46

Bruce eyed me disapprovingly from inside his little glass jar on the dashboard. He made an irritated **PING!** and a reply appeared on his LED screen.

WHAT DO YOU MEAN – AN EMERGENCY?
THIS IS AN AMBULANCE.
IT'S ALWAYS AN EMERGENCY.

The doctor *harrumphed*.

'This is a level one Q-T alert, Bruce,' she snapped. 'Fastest possible route to Cringetown high street!'

WE CAN'T GO THE FASTEST WAY.
ALL THE DIMENSION 5 SHORTCUTS ARE CLOSED.

'Closed?' said the doctor. 'Why?'

THE OLD GODS COMPLAINED ABOUT THE TRAFFIC.
SO THE COUNCIL IS INSTALLING SPEED BUMPS.

**'Blast!'** exclaimed the doctor. 'Then we'll never get to Cringetown before Inspector Pincher!'

Bruce's little wings fluttered when he heard this, and he made three excited **PINGS!**

WE COULD USE THE 'SLIGHTLY HAIRY'
DIMENSION AGAIN.
YOU KNOW HOW MUCH YOU ENJOYED IT LAST TIME.

His furry face suddenly displayed a lot of teeth, which I suspected was him smiling. The doctor thought for a moment, **shuddered,** but then reluctantly agreed. 'Oh, all right, then. It is an emergency.'

Bruce **wriggled happily** in his glass jar and made a *painfully high squeaking noise* that I suspected was his laugh. I didn't want to think about what the **'slightly hairy'** dimension was (or why Bruce thought it was so funny) so I asked the doctor who this Inspector Pincher was instead.

'The inspector is a member of the Q-T catcher squad,' she explained. 'A branch of the monster police made up of **brave monsters** and **things** who are prepared to risk their lives to protect the rest of us from toxic Q-Ts. But Pincher is a little more *driven* than most of the other catchers, I'm afraid, Ozzy.'

'In what way?' I asked. But before the doctor
could enlighten me Bruce sounded a **warning**
bell (actually, it was a ringtone of someone
being **violently sick**) and Lance the ambulance
swizzled into the **'SLIGHTLY HAIRY'** dimension.

Immediately, hair began to grow from **EVERYWHERE! My head, the backs of my hands, the inside of my nose.** It even began gushing out of my ears like a magician pulling silk scarves from his sleeve.

'AARGH!' I said. 'What's going on? I'm turning into my dad!'

'Don't panic!' said the doctor. 'It's all perfectly abnormal. Our hair will un-grow when we leave this stupid dimension. Well, most of it will.'

Bruce piped up with some advice.

Bruce may well be rude, egotistical, anti-social, mean-spirited and have a **twitchy,** irritable little face with close-set beady eyes, but he is an expert on coping with the **weird side-effects** of inter-dimensional travel. So I took his advice and asked the doctor to tell me more about Inspector Pincher. She was silent for a moment – not because she was thinking, though, but because an *impressive moustache-and-whiskers* combination was preventing her from speaking. So I waited while she pulled a comb from her jacket pocket and finally managed to uncover her mouth.

'When Percival Pincher was small,' she explained, 'he and a few of his fellow shrimplings got lost in the human world. This would have been dangerous enough as it was, but they also ran **slap-bang** into the dreaded *Miggimuss*.'

SUBJEC

AGE 8¾

CLASSIFIC

C–T (sub

Decapodula

REPORT

'Who's **Miggimuss?**' I asked.

'Oh, a legendary cutie,' she said. **'It's twenty feet tall, with big black ears, a bright red bottom and giant yellow pillows for feet. Ugh!** I feel ill just thinking about it. Anyway, Pincher and his poor hatch-mates barely survived the encounter. They lost several dozen legs between them, and poor Percival himself was struck completely dumb for six months! When he finally spoke again, his first words were a promise to **stamp out** all forms of *cuteness* from the monster world.'

'But that's ridiculous.' I laughed through my generous new moustache. 'You can't just get rid of attractiveness – at least not without allowing my mum to buy your clothes for you.'

The doctor sighed. 'Sadly you're right, young Ozzy. But it hasn't stopped Inspector Pincher and many of my fellow monsters from trying.'

I thought about this for a while, then a question occurred to me. 'If these cuties are so **eyeball-meltingly dangerous,** why are you in such a hurry to get close to one?'

'Remember the oath, Ozzy,' said the doctor.

**'"CURA OMNIA" – HEAL ANYTHING!** And that means *EVERY* intelligent creature. Be they monster, thing, ordinary – or even cutie. What if these **horrifically** *attractive* **creatures** are actually in pain? *What if their beauty is some kind of disease and they desperately need our help?'*

I hadn't thought of beauty being a desperate cry for help before. But I supposed if it were true it would certainly explain an awful lot about social media.

'Oh, and by the way,' continued the doctor as she furiously combed her **ever-increasing moustache** out of her mouth. 'Should we bump into Inspector Pincher, you would be wise to stay well out of his way.'

'**Why?**' I complained. 'What have I done?'

'Well, for one thing there is an undeniable amount of cuteness around your nasal area. And on top of that you are human! Pincher – and many other monsters, in fact – blame your kind for the *cutie problem* in the first place!'

'How on earth is cuteness our fault?' I protested. But there was no answer. The **vomiting ringtone** had sounded again.

The doctor's hands were back on the wheel and Lance had begun doing that deeply unpleasant thing that meant we were swizzling between the dimensions again.

And so I sat there trying to ignore the hair growing inside my skull by thinking very hard about Shao-Lin monks and the shiny top of my grandad's head.

# CRINGETOWN

## Chapter 7

After a few minutes, Lance dropped completely out of the 'slightly hairy' dimension.

There was an unpleasant moment of transition as all the extra hair was **sucked** back into my body like a high-speed film of someone eating spaghetti. An instant later, my hair was back to normal (i.e. no weirder than usual) and we were driving slowly down what looked like **a typical monster high street.**

So this was Cringetown.

It looked pretty much like an average human town, except there were a lot more **undertakers** and *snake-grooming parlours* than where I live.

And it was **completely** deserted.

There were grocery bags full of fish heads and freshly **baked loaves of dung bread** littering the pavements, but the residents were nowhere to be seen. Octa-cycles lay on the ground and hearses stood abandoned with their doors open, unattended coffins in the rear.

It looked as if the monsters of the town had been so terrified of whatever this **CUTIE** was that they'd abandoned everything and taken cover inside – just like the residents near my school every day at hometime.

We pulled up and parked outside **FANG-TASTIQUE FUN** – a monster toyshop that sold:

> # EVERYTHING FOR THE GRUMPY LITTLE MONSTER!
> - Un-cuddly toys
> - Inflatable coffins
> - Chain and padlock play-sets
> - Indoor explosives
> - The full range of PIERCE'S DIY horn kits

It was sandwiched between a **frozen drool-on-a-stick** parlour called *GARGLE-DAZ* and a monster florists called **MEAT YOUR PLANT,** which sold every imaginable kind of carnivorous plant. They were advertising a

> ## TRIFFID SALE: EVERYTHING MUST GO.
> **(PLEASE HELP YOURSELF!)**

'We'd better get in there quickly,' said the doctor as we climbed out of Lance. 'Who knows how long the Dimension 5 closure will delay Pincher.'

Had she just forgotten about the whole melting-eyeballs issue? In case she had, I raised it again. The doctor just sighed with disappointment.

'You really must stop being so **obsessed** with danger, Ozzy!' she chided. 'Danger is an **essential** part of discovering new cures for monsters. **A reckless disregard for personal safety is the hallmark of a good monster doctor.** That, of course, and the ability to run very, very fast.'

'But melting eyeballs?'

I tried one last time, hoping it was enough to end the argument.

'**Don't fret**, Nurse Ozzy!' she said. 'You personally won't come to any harm at all – for once. I will be taking all the risk, and –' she smiled as she pulled open Lance's back doors – '**I brought my very own protection!**'

There, swinging from a loading crane, was a riveted **metal globe** with a glass helmet. It was roughly the same size and shape as the monster doctor herself (i.e. spherical) and had jointed arms and legs fitted with **clampy** hands, like a cool **robot** from an ancient science-fiction film.

'An **anti-Q-T suit** of my own design!' she exclaimed proudly, and she whacked the suit's helmet with a crowbar. The crowbar bent. The helmet glass was about as thick as my *grandma's*  crossword glasses. 'My own patented anti-Q-T glass eliminates all Q-T radiation in the `1967.13 chesser-hertz wavelength`,' she said. I nodded knowledgeably. Like I do when my friends talk about cars or **reality-TV** programmes.

'**Marvellous.** Are you sure it will work?' I asked.

'Oh, almost certainly!' said the doctor. 'I wore it while reading one of your species' ghastly picture books. It was called *I WUV U MR SNUGGLE-WUGGLE*.\* Have you heard of it?'

I nodded, but it was much worse than that. I've listened to Mum and Dad read it to my little sister **5,387 times.**

\* *I WUV U MR SNUGGLE-WUGGLE* is the story of a furry pink blob who gets separated from his owner (the simpering Celia) in the soft-furnishings section of a major department store. After a 'thrilling' adventure involving lazy cushions, an annoying table lamp called Blinky and a surprisingly clever footstool, he is reunited with Celia. Hugs are given. Lessons are learned. Vomit is held back.

'Well,' she continued, 'I got through the whole thing, cover to cover, without **vomiting,** facial burns or any temporary blindness at all. In fact, I had nothing worse than a mild headache!' She pressed a catch and the suit split open at the waist, like the two halves of a chocolate **Easter egg.** She climbed into the lower half easily, but when the top half dropped down it got stuck.

**'BLAST!'** she cursed. 'It must have shrunk in the wash! **Don't just stand there, Ozzy!** Give me a hand!'

I won't go into detail about the next few minutes of getting the doctor into the anti-Q-T suit, other than to say it involved:

• Me jumping up and down on her head.

• The doctor doing something **horribly unnatural**

with her left shoulder.

• A lot of words in languages I didn't understand, but still sounded **rude.**

Eventually there was a loud **POP!**, she said, **'OW!** That got it!' and the suit clicked into place. The doctor put the helmet on and began windmilling her arms and doing deep knee bends like the teacher of an **astronaut aerobics class.** She pointed to a large box. 'Grab the Q-T-containment box and be ready! We'd better get a move on before that **blasted** inspector arrives to stick his interfering mandibles in everything!'

The box had wheels and a long handle, and was made of the same metal as the suit.

'That will hold the cutie securely,' she explained. 'And also protect **decent monsters** from being exposed to any deadly radiation. So when I grab the cutie make sure you're ready and waiting with the box!' Then, without further ado, she **stomped** off across the street in the direction of **FANG-TASTIQUE FUN.**

I watched her go, wondering whether she was **completely fearless or completely mad.** But as usual I couldn't tell. My stomach seemed to be working its way through *The Bumper Book of Knots* as she pushed open the front door with the suit's claw.

But then she paused in the doorway.

Had she seen something inside?

She turned and shouted over her shoulder,

**'GET A MOVE ON, OZZY! I'M GOING TO NEED THAT BOX IN A MINUTE. IT WON'T BE ANY USE TO ME OVER THERE NOW, WILL IT?'**

What?

She didn't seriously expect me to follow her, did she? I thought she was supposed to be taking all the risk this time! I snapped out of my shock and bellowed back at her, **'I DON'T HAVE A Q-T SUIT!'** But it was too late. She had disappeared inside.

What was I supposed to do now?

I didn't want my eyeballs to melt! I liked my eyeballs the way they were (i.e. on either side of my nose and not running down my cheeks).

But how bad would I feel if something awful happened to the doctor and I wasn't there to help? How would I explain to the owner of **The Battered Squid** chippy (Simon the six-headed salamander) that I'd let his best customer come to harm? And, even worse than that, what on earth would I tell my mum and dad if they found out that I hadn't helped someone when I could have?

There was nothing for it. I grabbed the handle of the **Q-T-containment box** and hurried over to the door of **FANG-TASTIQUE FUN.**

I carefully nudged it open with the toe of one shoe – in case it had been contaminated by the cutie – then I took a deep breath,

pulled my **CURA OMNIA** T-shirt over my head to protect my eyes, **mustered my courage** and stepped very cautiously inside.

# BIT WEIRD TO QUITE SHOCKING

## Chapter 8

'Are you coming in, or not?' snapped the doctor.
I peered through the fabric of my T-shirt and
could see her pulling toys off shelves. '**I know** it's
hiding in here somewhere!'

'If it's all the same to you,' I answered, 'I'd
**rather** stay over here by the door and not see my
eyeballs melt!' The doctor sighed. She **stomped**

over to the vampire toddler section and swept fake **fangs**, plastic **capes**, rubber **stakes** and bouncy balls painted to look like garlic cloves to the floor.

'Don't be so ridiculous, Ozzy,' she said. 'How on earth could you "see" your own eyeballs melt? That doesn't make any sense! Anyway, did O&N say anything about how **ordinaries** are affected by cuties?'

I realized that the book hadn't mentioned ordinaries at all. 'And that, my young apeling, is because your entire **bizarre** species is immune to cuties,' she explained. 'In fact, you are not just immune – you seem to be in *love* with them! You humans are forever creating stories and images about cute things. My goodness, you even have entire companies devoted to inventing the *cutest* thing your disordered brains can imagine. Which,' she added, 'the monster community considers to be in **extremely poor taste indeed.**'

I pulled the T-shirt back down, feeling a little **stupid** now.

'The truth is, Ozzy, that you're almost certainly safer stood right next to a cutie than you are at meal times with your baby sister.' She was certainly right about that. You'd be amazed at the pain that child can inflict with a **well-aimed rusk.**

'Now that you know your precious eyeballs are safe,' she chided, 'can you *please* stop worrying and remember that Pincher could arrive at **any** moment?' The doctor pulled a small device from her suit's utility belt and started to scan the room with it. **'Q-T detector,'** she explained. 'Measures Q-T particles.' As she waved it back and forth across the shop, it made the same soft BEEP! no matter what it was pointed at. I glanced over at the gauge. The indicator needle quivered gently towards the right-hand side of some kind of *cuteness scale.**

\* In case you're interested, it's known as Potter-Poe's Q-T Scale.

For more information and examples of the various classifications of the Q-T Scale, see the relevant section in *Ogbert & Nish*. Or just randomly browse any social-media platform for an hour or so.

'Strange!' said the doctor. 'I should be picking up some

pretty strong Q-T radiation by now. But I'm not getting anything **dangerously** *attractive* at all.'

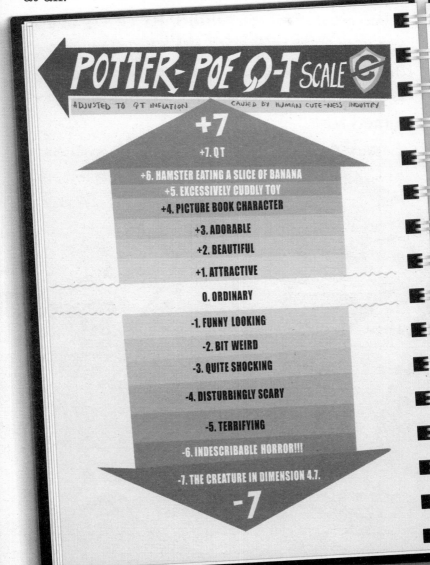

She pointed the device at me for a second.
There was a little hum and the needle twitched to
**'BIT WEIRD'.** Then it flickered to **'ATTRACTIVE',**
before settling around **'ORDINARY'.** Every now
and then it would give a random little twitch to
the left and right of the scale.

'Hmmm . . . It seems to working,' she mused.
'Perhaps it just needs **careful recalibration.**' She
banged it hard against the edge of a shelf (several
times) before sweeping it once more around the
room. But the needle stayed firmly stuck in the
middle somewhere between **'BIT WEIRD'** and
**'ATTRACTIVE'.**

'What's wrong with this **stupid thing?**
According to this, there's nothing in here apart
from **good, honest, scary monster
merchandise.** Not a trace of Q-T
radiation at all. That can't be right!'
she growled. **'New-fangled
rubbish!'** And she tossed
the meter away.

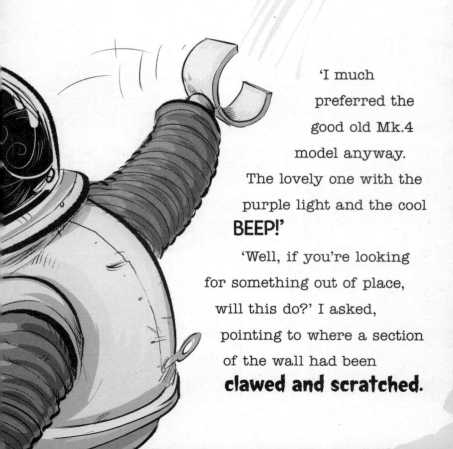

'I much
preferred the
good old Mk.4
model anyway.
The lovely one with the
purple light and the cool
**BEEP!'**
'Well, if you're looking
for something out of place,
will this do?' I asked,
pointing to where a section
of the wall had been
**clawed and scratched.**

The plaster was torn away, exposing the brickwork beneath.

'**By the triple-twisting tongue twisters of Nasty Nigel Nimnitz!**' the doctor exclaimed. 'The cutie must have tried to escape through there.'

I didn't understand. 'Why? Surely that only leads to a shop selling **man-eating plants.** Why would the cutie risk going in there?'

'Who can tell what goes through the minds of *attractive* beings,' the doctor said as she knelt for a closer look at the damaged plaster. 'But it clearly failed. Which means it must still be in here . . . **somewhere.**' She looked around suspiciously before **clanking off** across the shop, peering into every display bin and checking every shelf while muttering, 'Keep your eyes peeled for anything cute.'

I spotted a large display basket full of what were marked as **'UN-CUDDLIES'.** It was full of toys that would have given an ordinary child nightmares. The one on top was a very **ugly hairy werewolf** called:

WULFi

HE'S HAIRY! HE'S FUNNY! HE'S HIL-HAIRY-OUS!

**Ugh!** Not cute at all. The one beneath that was even worse. **Yeuch!** I dropped that one quickly.

But at least the one below it seemed a bit less scary. For one thing, it had nice pale-blue fur that didn't seem that

hideous. I picked it up for a closer look. It was actually no more scary than a **slightly cross-looking teddy bear** with too many teeth. I held it up to the doctor.

'See!' I said. 'Monsters aren't **that** different to ordinaries, Doctor. In fact this toy isn't hideous at all! What do you call this creature? There's no label.'

The doctor was busy rummaging through a bin of light-proof sleeping bags for **VAMPIRES,** but she paused and looked up briefly. Then she **froze,** her face turning bright green with shock.

**'STAND STILL!'** she hissed. **'DO! NOT! MOVE!'**

The doctor must have spotted the cutie. But where on earth was it? My head swivelled around the room, looking for it.

**'Nurse Ozzy?'** said the doctor. **'I . . . want . . . you . . . to . . . try . . . and . . . stay . . . veeeeerrrrry . . . calm!'** She began to approach as cautiously as she could manage in that **clanky** Q-T suit. The claw hands were outstretched as she whispered, 'Just take a **DEEP** breath and think of something very calming – like wearing a hot-water bottle on your head while eating a plate of warm worms in toffee sauce. And try very, **VERY, VERY** hard not to panic.'

'Panic?' I was confused. Where was this cutie? 'Why on earth would I panic?'

The doctor edged closer. She spoke slowly and carefully, as if I were a curious toddler who had found a fully working **flame-thrower**.

'Because that **"thing"** you are holding . . .' she said, in a slow and careful voice, 'is the cutie.'

'Don't be ridiculous!' I laughed. 'This little

thing is harmless. In fact –' I pulled it nearer and gazed into its rather *charming* little face. *It had large, open eyes, a tiny button nose and the sweetest little mouth.* 'It's actually really, really—'

'**CUTE!**' hissed the doctor.

And just as she said that very word the thing in my hands blinked and its face transformed.

The teeth disappeared. Its beady eyes grew wide and soft and kind. It smiled sweetly at me and squeaked like a *baby kitten* tasting double cream for the first time. All at once I felt like

one of those **funny chocolate puddings** that go all melty when you cut into them. The little creature I held before me looked so *perfectly* innocent and defenceless. It obviously needed me to look after it, protect it, and – most important of all – give it lots and lots of hugs. I smiled down at that perfect little face. It smiled back and **wriggled** its cute nose. My heart did the weird chocolate-pudding thing again and some part of my brain I hadn't known I possessed went, **Awwwwwwwww!**

'Who's a clever little—?' I began, but before I could finish the sentence the doctor made a **lunge** for the cutie. I swung it out of her reach and her suit's clunky metal claws snapped shut on nothing.

'**WHAT ON EARTH ARE YOU DOING?**' I protested. 'You might have hurt it!'

'**SNAP OUT OF IT, NURSE!**' the doctor barked, and she made another grab for my precious bundle of gorgeousness. But this time I raised the cutie high above my head. The doctor **hopped** up and down, snapping away frantically, but she was too short to reach it. Nearby, a really annoying tinny alarm was going off.

**'You don't understand,'** the doctor pleaded. 'You are under its *malign influence.* Look at the Q-T meter!' She pointed to where the battered box lay. It was the source of the annoying alarm. 'The Q-T readings are hitting **+5** and rising! Give the creature to me at once! It needs to be placed in confinement. For goodness' sake! It's **not** a toy!'

But I wasn't going to let anyone take away my little cutie.

'All right, then,' said the doctor. 'But, just remember, I'm doing this for your own good!'

Then she **kicked** me very hard in the left shin.

# M.U.S.H.

## Chapter 9

'**O**W!' I shrieked, and I grabbed my shin, dropping the cutie in the process. The doctor caught it neatly with one metal pincer, **flipped** the containment box open with the other and – with a look of complete **disgust** – dropped the cutie quickly inside.

She **slammed** the lid shut and the Q-T meter's alarm cut off. The **gooey** feeling in my chest also disappeared like somebody had turned off a radio playing my favourite song.

'**Um,** what just happened to my brain?' I asked.

'I apologize for striking you,' she said, while securing the lock on the box. 'But you were under the **cutie's influence.** You ordinaries may not be injured by cuteness, but you aren't **entirely** unaffected. If one of your species spends too much time around something emitting Q-T radiation, your brain slowly turns to what we in the monster doctor profession call '**M.U.S.H.**' or **Mind Under Soppy Hypnosis.** Long-term exposure can have **horrific** effects in ordinaries.*

* M.U.S.H. SYMPTOMS Recent research by Professor Twinky Hornscreamer at the University of East Ugglia has shown that Q-T radiation affects the speech centres of ordinaries' brains. Early symptoms can be diagnosed in speech defects like 'little' becoming 'lickle', 'clever' becoming 'cwever', and so on. Eventually, intelligent speech fails completely and the subject can only create simple sounds like 'goo-goo', 'ga-ga' and 'choo-choo'. Brain death (level 1) follows soon after.

COMPLETE MUSH

But never mind that,' the doctor said, practically bouncing up and down with excitement now. 'This creature, Ozzy! **Oh my word!** We need to get it back to the surgery as quickly as possible. **Hurry up!'** She clanked out of the shop and headed towards Lance, wheeling the Q-T-containment box behind her. I followed, trying to keep up while still rubbing my shin.

'This is an **extraordinary** discovery,' she exclaimed. 'This **marvellous** creature . . .' she paused to actually bend down and *kiss* the box, 'is able to turn its Q-T emissions up or down – completely at will. Imagine that! One moment you were as intelligent as an ordinary ever can be, and mere seconds later your brain was turned into total **M.U.S.H.** by the Q-T emissions. Incredible!'

I didn't see what **M.U.S.H.** had to do with melted eyeballs. 'So monsters aren't actually in any danger?' I asked.

**'No, no, no!'** replied the doctor as we arrived back at Lance. 'But if we can just work out how this creature masks its **toxic** cuteness we might be able to create technologies to block the **deadly nature of the Q-T effect** completely.

Imagine, **anti-Q-T spectacles or anti-Q-T foil hats!**

**Heavens!** Monsters, things and cuties might finally be able to coexist with each other. We might even be able to finally forgive humans for the **I WUV U MR SNUGGLE-WUGGLE** film series – even **I WUV U MR SNUGGLE-WUGGLE 5: FROM HUGS TO ETERNITY.**

I thought that might be a bit far-fetched. The fifth **Snuggle** film is an **abomination** of cuteness. But I kept quiet as we stowed the Q-T box in the rear of Lance and climbed back in.

'*Thank goodness* we found it before that ghastly Pincher arrived,' she mused. Then she addressed the BAT-NAV. 'Home, please, Bruce.'

## CAN WE GO BACK VIA THE—?

'**No,**' she said, very firmly. 'I've had quite enough hair growth for one day. And that last trip has given me a **terrible itch** in my—'

Bruce fluttered his disapproval, but Lance gave three low revs of his engine (which is how he laughs) and we *rocketed* off down Cringeton high street.

We were soon travelling at a speed somewhere between '**losing your licence**' and '**lifetime imprisonment**'.

My head was **PINNED** straight back against the headrest so that all I could see was the windscreen dead ahead, which had some **weird** kind of bug stuck to it. It was very faint and had a sort of *sparkly shimmery glow* around it. A bit like the glow that Lance sometimes has around him.

**Weirder still,** it seemed to be getting clearer. No. That couldn't be right.

I suddenly realized it wasn't a bug at all. It was **another inter-dimensional vehicle** and it was emerging from a jump **dead-ahead** in the middle of Cringetown high street – **and we were heading straight for it!**

I looked over to see if the doctor had noticed it but – **to my horror** – she wasn't even steering! Instead, she'd popped the top of the anti-Q-T suit off and was busy **scratching furiously.**

I looked back to the windscreen. The thing was solid enough now to be identifiable as a large police wagon. Unfortunately there was no way it would see us until it fully arrived – **but we would crash straight into it before that!**

So, without asking permission, I grabbed the steering wheel and **yanked** it hard left. Lance skidded round the corner and, for one horrifying moment, he was as **dangerously** out of control as my auntie Ingrid *dancing* to ABBA.

The ambulance spun **round and round and round,** more times than I cared for, before it finally came to a stop in a narrow lane just off the high street.

'**Ozzy,**' said the doctor after she had
extracted herself from the footwell. 'While that
was **enormous** fun, was there a point to it
at all?'

By way of an answer I pointed to where the **HUGE** (and very shiny) police wagon was rolling slowly past the end of the side street. It was heading towards **FANG-TASTIQUE FUN** and the lettering down its side was clearly visible.

Luckily, its driver was so intent on getting to his destination that he didn't even glance down our alley. I did get a really good look at him, though.

Even by the **usually horrid standards** of monsterness he was **extremely monsterish.**

He was basically lobster-like, with a shell the same luminous angry scarlet as Dad's **hideous sunburn**  from last summer. He was gripping the steering wheel with two large – AND VERY SHARP-LOOKING – claws. With an assortment of smaller pincers, he was busy tweaking mirrors, fiddling with the radio and adjusting the air-con. He had the same permanently annoyed look that my geography teacher, Mr Peevish, has.

'HA HA!' giggled the doctor. 'Not this time, Percy Pincher!' Then she added, 'Take us home, please, Bruce,' and resumed her scratching.

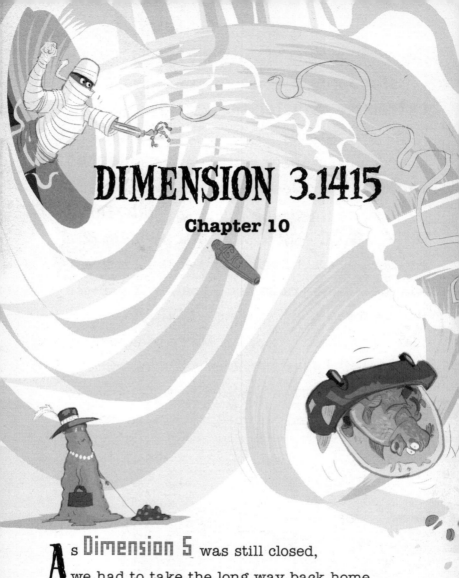

# DIMENSION 3.1415

## Chapter 10

As Dimension 5 was still closed, we had to take the long way back home. Lance jumped from the roof of the **17.15 from Hamburg** to the undiscovered tomb of the **Pharaoh Ra-Man** via a deserted Pacific atoll.

But finally we **corkscrewed** down through a nice, quiet bit of *swoosy-wooshy* nothingness and back into Lovecraft Avenue.

We both hopped out and Lance trundled off to his garage for a well-deserved **splash-about** in his oil bath.

'Listen,' the doctor said. 'I'll go and give **Professor Twinky Hornscreamer** at the University of East Ugglia a call. He's an expert on all things *cute* and **dangerously** *attractive*. He'll know where to store the cutie safely. Meanwhile, you stash it somewhere nice and quiet.' She thought for a moment. 'Somewhere no one else would dare go . . . **Ha!** Delores's booth! No one would be stupid enough to go in there after Trevor's carry-on this morning.'

'Er . . . what about Trevor?' I asked. 'Isn't he still dangerous?'

'Oh no,' said the doctor. 'He'll be as good as gold by now. Triffids are **marvellous** houseplants as long as you feed and water them correctly, and don't mind the occasional pet or **slow-moving relative** going missing.'

REWARD

Missing Monster
LAST SEEN WORKING
IN GREENHOUSE.
VANISHED WITHOUT A TRACE!
Call 7070707-0707704
Wingbolton Squidlick

But, when I got inside, Delores wasn't at all keen on the doctor's idea. She peered at the cutie box with a look of **disgust** that was even stronger than her usual one.

'Isn't it contagious?' she asked suspiciously.

'Isn't what contagious?' I said.

'*Cuteness, of course!*' she replied. 'My uncle Scrofulus used to swear till he was **orange in the face** that you can catch cuteness from a cutie.' She held a compact mirror up to her blobby face and puckered her **blubbery** green lips. **'Ugh!** The thought of losing all my horrible looks!'

'But the doctor said it's only for a while,' I protested. 'Someone called Dr Twinky is coming over to—'

'Dr Twinky?' interrupted Delores. And her face began to contort in a **really odd** way. The edges of her mouth seemed to be trying to get off her face and climb inside her ears.

It took me a few moments to realize that **she was trying to smile.** (I'd never seen Delores smile properly before. And, to be honest, I don't really want to ever again.)

'Oh, why didn't you say that before?' she said. 'I'd do **anything** for Dr Twinky. He did such a *lovely job* removing that whaling harpoon from my husband's head after that **terrible mix-up** at the beach. I'll pop the kettle on and put out a plate of those biscuits I know he likes – the ones with the **rum-soaked flies** in.'* She slithered off to the kitchen and I slipped into her booth.

* IMPORTANT INFO
There are two biscuit tins in the monster doctor's surgery. Mine is the one that doesn't contain rum-soaked beetle-bites, baked blisters or caramel cockroaches!
YOU HAVE BEEN WARNED!

DELORES
BISCUITS

OZZY's
BISCUITS

Delores' ↑          mine ↑

The doctor had been right about Trevor the triffid. He was just sitting there in his pot, looking about as dangerous as a **floret of broccoli.** So I rolled the confinement box underneath Delores's desk, checked it was locked and pulled down all the blinds to keep out prying eyes. Then I locked the booth door, pocketed the key and breathed a *sigh of relief.*

I was just thinking about having a cup of tea and a biscuit myself when the most **awful** noise came from the street outside.

It went

WAARG-OOO-WAAARRGH

WAARGHH-OOOHHH-WAARGHH

# OO-ARGHH!

and sounded like some kind of crazy
siren. (Either that or my dad had found
the karaoke machine again.)

'What is that **dreadful racket?**' I asked,
just as the doctor rushed out of her office. We both
reached the window to the street just in time to
see the massive **Q-T catcher wagon**, driven
by the dreaded Inspector Pincher, screech to a
halt outside.

**'Ah,'** said the doctor. 'This could be a little
awkward.'

# INSPECTOR PINCHER

## Chapter 11

$\mathcal{T}$hankfully, someone turned the awful siren off. But the horrible flashing lights on top of the **Q-T catcher wagon** stayed on. They strobed painfully between **infra-purple** and **violent-green** (which in my opinion is a disgusting choice of colours).

They were so bright that I could even see them with my eyes closed! This was deeply unpleasant – but it also reminded me of something I had read recently about flashing lights.

**Now what was it?** It had seemed very important at the time . . .

I lost my train of thought as the driver's door on the big vehicle flew open and Inspector Pincher *scuttled* out.

Up this close I could see that his face sported a wide moustache of wriggling mandibles that looked like a line of **dancing worms.**

'SERGEANT HAWIET!' he said – or, rather, sprayed. Speaking seemed to involve a **disturbing** amount of saliva – on account of the mandibles I supposed. 'I want gwound zewo sealed off as **tight as a dwum!** Nothing gets in or out! Put the bawwiers over THERE, THERE and THERE!' He jabbed his pincers around like a self-important air steward pointing out the emergency exits.

Sergeant Hawiet (or Hairiet as I suspected she was called) was covered in thick grey fur and had **curly little horns** growing from where her head probably was. She began to unload the barriers about as enthusiastically as I take homework out of my backpack. She had a single large eye, which she **rolled** at Pincher several times. I got the impression that she couldn't stand him.

'HUWWY UP, Sergeant!' Pincher continued. 'SNAP SNAP! The Q-T must not get away. And fetch me my megaphone.' Pincher clicked one of his huge claws like a rude customer summoning a waiter. Hairiet sighed heavily, stopped setting up the barriers and passed the megaphone to Pincher. He raised it to his **blubbery** lips.

**'ATTENTION INSIDE THE SURGEWY!'** he announced. **'I know you're in there, Annie. I thought I saw your GWUBBY little ambulance fleeing Cwingetown earlier. But my suspicions were confirmed when I found stwange twaces of Q-T radiation in the shop – but no sign of any cweature! So, imagine my surpwise when I DISCOVERED –'** he dramatically reached into a pocket to produce a familiar-looking box – **'THIS!'**

It was, unmistakeably, the Q-T meter the doctor had discarded earlier. I recognized all the heavy dents from where she'd tried to 'recalibrate' it back in the shop.

'OOPS,' said the doctor.

'**Interfering with official Q–T catcher business is a VEWY sewious offence, Annie. I suggest you come out immediately before I am forced to come in there AND AWWEST YOU!'**

To show that he meant business, the inspector brandished a **fearsome**-looking weapon. It looked like a cross between **a shotgun, a rocket launcher and a badly bent garden fork.***

* Clipping from the VON-PUNSCH weapons catalogue

Suddenly, a pounding noise filled the surgery.

*THUMP!*
*THUMP-THUMP!*
*THUMP! THUMP-THUMP! THUMP!*

For a moment I thought the inspector was **actually trying** to break down the surgery's front door, but I was wrong. The **THUMPING** was coming from behind me – inside the **surgery!**

It stopped for a second, but then began again.

*THUMP!*
*THUMP-THUMP!*
*THUMP! THUMP-THUMP! THUMP!*

This time it was accompanied by the equally loud scraping of something heavy being dragged (or dragging itself) across the floor.

**'DELORES!'** yelled the doctor. **'Can you not manage to make TEA a little more QUIETLY THAN THAT? We're trying to—'**

'*What are you talking about?*' said the receptionist. She had just emerged from the kitchen carrying the **very** battered tea tray from earlier, which now held cups of hot steaming bilge tea and some **menacing-looking** *biscuits*.

This was a little worrying. (And not just because of the biscuits.) If Delores wasn't making the noise, **then what was?**

There was nothing back there apart from the tiny little cutie in Delores's receptionist booth and the –

**'OH NO!'**

I suddenly remembered what was important about flashing lights. **'THE EMERGENCY LIGHTS!'** I blurted. They were still flashing outside.

'The lights, Ozzy?' asked the doctor. 'The colours are a bit **tacky,** certainly. **But pull yourself together!** This is no time to get all artsy on me. We have other things to—'

**'HOMICIDAL RAGE!'** I exclaimed, and pointed to Delores's booth. Something in there was **hammering** on the other side of the door, trying to get out. **'TREVOR THE TRIFFID! FLASHING INFRA-VIOLET LIGHTS! DESTROY ALL LIFE ON EARTH!'** I may have said in a **slightly screamy** way.

The doctor realized what I was talking about* and her pupils did a **panicky** little dance around the whites of her eyes.

'By **my brother's badly blistered bald bottoms,'** she cried. 'You're right! Trevor **MUST** have seen Pincher's emergency lights and has gone all homicidal on us! Well, this is awkward!

We can't afford a homicidal-triffid incident today –
*especially* since I believe the pharmacy is fresh
out of therapeutic nuclear weapons.'

'OPEN UP AT WONCE IN THE NAME OF
THE Q–T SQUAD!' blubbered the outraged and
very wet voice of Inspector Pincher from outside.

# 'MY PATIENCE IS WEARING THIN, DOCTOR!'

The doctor flung the front window wide open and *bellowed* out into the street, **'DO YOU MIND, PERCIVAL? WE'VE GOT A BIT OF A TRIFFID SITUATION IN HERE. SO I WOULD APPRECIATE A BIT OF PATIENCE!'**

Then she slammed the window closed so hard the glass fell out.

## THUMP!
## THUMP-THUMP!
## THUMP! THUMP-THUMP! THUMP!

The doctor and I both looked up at the tiny window above the door of Delores's booth and my heart **instantly** fell. For there, behind the frosted glass, were the shadows of **triffid tendrils** whipping furiously around inside.

To make matters worse, the noise of the **dreadful** vegetable was suddenly joined by the **BANG! BANG! BANG! BANG!** of someone hammering on the surgery's front door.

It seemed that Pincher's already thin patience had finally run out. 'OPEN UP AT ONCE!' he threatened. 'Or I shall be forced to VAPOUWISE this DOOR!'

We were now stuck between a **crabby** government inquisitor with a big gun and a homicidal plant. I was thinking I should maybe have taken Dad's advice and got a paper round for my summer job when the doctor spoke.

**'I've got a plan,'** she announced confidently.

I breathed a sigh of relief. She would know what to do.

'I'm afraid there's nothing for it,' she said. 'We can't tackle Trevor on our own. Ozzy, *kindly* **show Inspector Pincher in.'**

# WIDICULOUS!

## Chapter 12

Pincher stood in the open doorway looking **jolly** annoyed. But before he could complain about being kept waiting the doctor was doing what she did best – **talking very fast and waving her hands around a lot.**

'Listen, Pincher,' she blurted. 'I understand you're upset, but let's just put a pin in the whole cutie "misunderstanding" for one moment. I'm afraid we have a homicidal triffid situation here and could really use your hel—'

Three of Pincher's smaller pincers grabbed the doctor's lips and **squeezed** them tightly shut, like the edges of a Cornish pasty. She was unable to speak.

'I don't have time for your no doubt **highly amusing** stowy!' said Pincher. 'I cannot hear any twiffid!'

He was right. **Alas,** Trevor had chosen that exact moment to finish his vegetable drum solo.

*'But it's true!'* I said, trying to look as honest as I possibly could. Auntie Wilhelmina always said that you can go a long way by looking honest. (But then she was currently in prison for robbing a bank, so perhaps her advice should be taken with a **pinch of salt.**)

Inspector Pincher's stalky eyes swivelled and seemed to notice me for the very first time. A **Mexican wave of** disgust shivered across his mandibles.

'So it is twue!' Pincher sneered. 'I had heard the rumours, of course. But really, Dr Sichertall! Employing an **ORDINARY!** Do you not care about your reputation? This . . .' He shook his head in disgust at me. 'This . . . this . . . **"cweature"** is *completely un-monstrous!'* He turned to his harassed assistant and snapped, **'SERGEANT!** Have you found that foul Q-T yet?'

Poor Sergeant Hairiet had slunk in behind

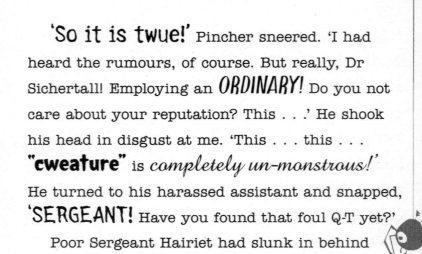

her boss and was busy scanning the surgery with a Q-T meter.

'I'm getting the same reading as back in Cringetown, sir,' she said. 'But I can't find a source for it in the surgery.'

'**Widiculous!**' snapped Pincher, and snatched the meter from her. '**Give ME that!** You're obwiously weeding it all wrong!' He jabbed it around the surgery at random, but Hairiet had been right. They couldn't pinpoint the Q-T's location. Presumably the Q-T-confinement box was doing its job (or the clever little creature had turned its charms off). '**What is wong with this thing?**' he cried. 'It must be faulty.' The doctor, still unable to speak, tried to **mime** something very complicated with her arms.

Pincher's curiosity got the better of him and he released his pincers from the doctor's lips and barked, 'WHAT?'

'Look at my meter,' she said. It was hanging from Pincher's belt and the Q-T readings were **identical.** 'There's nothing wrong with yours. The cutie was gone when we arrived in Cringetown. And it's not here either!'

'Pah!' snapped Pincher. He didn't believe the doctor (who – to be fair – was actually lying) and continued **jabbing** his meter at everything in the surgery, in the vain hope of finding a trace of the cutie.

**'You're wasting your time!'** said the doctor as she tried to rub some circulation back into her lips. 'There's nothing attractive in my surgery. But **really,** Inspector, we do still need your help with this homicidal triff—'

'I've had enough of your twicks, Doctor!' Pincher interrupted. 'WHERE IS THE CUTIE?' he demanded, spraying saliva all over her. He grabbed my arm with one of his smaller pincers. 'This is your last chance, Annie! Tell me WIGHT NOW! Or I awwest your assistant on a charge of having a suspiciously attwactive nasal appendage.'

I didn't like the sound of that. Or the **smell** of it either! Pincher's breath was as **fishy** as the bins behind **The Battered Squid** chippy. He was just starting to pull me towards the door when, in the nick of time, Trevor decided to strike up his **beat-box** routine again.

# THUMP! THUMP-THUMP!
# THUMP! THUMP-THUMP! THUMP!

'What's that?' cried Sergeant Hairiet.

'AHA!' cried the inspector **triumphantly.** 'It's the Q-T!' He pushed me aside, scuttled across to Delores's booth and pressed his head to the door. The thrashing around inside was growing **louder** every second. '**QUICK,** Sergeant.

**Hand me my helmet!** It's **TWYING** to get away again! We saw what it could do to walls back in Cwingeton!' Then he rounded on the doctor, snicked his claws menacingly and demanded, 'Give me the key for this door, **IMMEDIATELY!**'

'I can't let you harm—' said the doctor.

**'Disgusting!'** shrieked Pincher. He was outraged. 'You care more for these *attwactive* **cweatures** than you do for your own fellow monsters.'

'Actually,' replied the doctor, 'I was going to say "I can't let you harm yourself". But since you're so **determined** to do it anyway . . .' She handed Pincher the key.

'What on earth are you doing?' I asked, but the doctor just shrugged. (Which is a complicated gesture involving her **shoulders, knees** and **ears** and can easily be mistaken for the opening steps of an Irish jig.)

'If the inspector wants to enter a tiny room with a **homicidal triffid,**' she explained, 'then who am I to stand in his way?'

Pincher smiled **victoriously** and inserted the key into the lock.

'Er . . . Inspector,' I tried one more time. 'That thing in there **really is a triffid.**'

'Called Trevor,' added Delores, who had taken a seat in the reception area and was noisily sipping tea and munching biscuits. She was determined not to miss the inspector getting **eaten** by a homicidal Trevor.

'Please, sir,' said Sergeant Hairiet. 'Perhaps you should listen to the doctor. She is very knowledg—'

'**Nonsense!**' snorted Pincher. He was absolutely convinced he was dealing with a cutie. So we watched as he lowered his protective helmet, readied the gun-fork thing and, without further ado, *scuttled* through the door to Delores's booth.

The doctor immediately **slammed** it shut behind him. Delores, Sergeant Hairiet and I joined her at the door just in time to hear the inspector's last words,

120

which consisted of, 'GET BACK! GET BACK OR I'LL SHOO—' before his voice was drowned out by the most **unpleasant noise** I've ever heard.

It was the sound of Trevor eating him.

# CIRCLE OF LIFE

## Chapter 13

How to describe the noise?

Our dog, **Piglet,** doesn't have much in the way of table manners. I once watched him eat an unattended whole plate of **spaghetti Bolognese.** (Don't ask. It was an experiment.) He didn't so much 'eat' the spaghetti as **breathe** it in through his nose, **lick it up,** smear it all over his face and then *sneeze* out any leftover bits.

**Then he ate those bits all over again.**

It was **horrible** to listen to and (trust me) much worse to watch. But the sound of Trevor the triffid eating Inspector Pincher was even **worse.**

Eventually, there was a brief moment of silence. Then Delores unwrapped a *chocolate-covered* **beetle bar** from her pocket and began chomping noisily. The doctor looked at her pointedly.

'What?' asked Delores. 'I was feeling hungry!'

'Do try and show some *respect,*' said the doctor. 'We may not have liked the inspector, but that doesn't mean we wanted to hear him being eaten by a triffid. And, if we did, perhaps not while we were standing in the room next door.'

She turned to me and put a huge arm round my shoulders. 'Ozzy, I know ordinaries are sensitive about this sort of thing, but you must remember it is **Monster**-*Mother Nature's way*,' she explained. 'The spider eats the fly. The bird eats the spider. The homicidal triffid eats the **annoying** government employee.'

'Circle of life,' muttered Delores as she swallowed the last of the beetle bar and opened a packet of **deep-fried toenail clippings.** She began to crunch them noisily too.

## MINISTRY OF MONSTER

### HEALTH + UNSANITATION DEPT

Outbreak notice: #54-BXXX
(Triffid)
PENALTIES
* Failure to report a triffid outbreak (homicidal) is punishable by up to 800 years in a maximum-security concrete box or a fine of 7,000,000 Karlofz – whichever is more annoying at the time.

'I'm going to have to report this to **head office** immediately, Doc,' said Sergeant Hairiet. 'You know the rules about **triffid outbreaks.** We'll have to start the evacuation immediately.' Her large eye suddenly looked **very serious** indeed, which was odd as you'd have thought the recent digestion of her boss would have cheered her up a bit.

'Of course,' said the doctor. She picked up her favourite mug and started to walk towards the door.

'Thank you, Doctor,' said the sergeant. 'But there's no need to hurry. It'll take **head office** a few hours to write out a prescription for the atomic sterilizing kit. And it shouldn't be necessary to **"treat"** more than the surgery up to

The Battered Squid.'

'Wait, what?' I asked disbelievingly. 'You're going to set off an atomic bomb inside the surgery?'

'Only a tiny one,' said Sergeant Hairiet somewhat defensively. 'I admit that it might seem a bit harsh to a *non-monster*, but, trust me, you can't take any chances with a triffid once it has tasted monster flesh.'

'Hang on . . .' I said, turning to the doctor. 'If we're supposed to **"TREAT ANYTHING"**, then why do we drop atomic bombs on homicidal triffids? Don't they deserve our care?'

She shook her head sadly. 'I'm afraid, Ozzy, there are some creatures we just cannot save. **Triffids, gross-flatulators**ᵀ and *TV panel-show guests* are all beyond the tools of modern monster medicine. For instance, right now Trevor is busily turning himself into a **triffid seed bomb.** Sometime tomorrow, he will **explode** and scatter millions of homicidal **mini-Trevors** up into the stratosphere and then all across the surface of the world. The authorities will never be able to hunt them all down in time. It'll be worse than **the great boy-band**ᵀ **plague** of the last century.'

This seemed ridiculous to me since there wasn't a peep coming from the room next door. So I made a suggestion.

* Dimension 3.9 is the dimensional version of that area round the back of everyone's house where they keep all the broken stuff. You know, that spot just out of sight of both the kitchen window and the garden where there is:

- A mould-covered set of mismatched garden furniture.
- Bits of bicycles you don't ever remember buying.
- Something greenish and sort of alive in an old margarine tub.

'Before anyone sets off an atomic bomb – however small – shouldn't we **at least** have a quick peek inside the booth? Perhaps Trevor's just **stuffed** and sleeping off a big meal. If he is, then maybe we could bundle him into Lance and drop him somewhere he can't do any harm – like Dimension 3.9?'*

The doctor, Sergeant Hairiet and Delores all looked at each other for a moment. I watched as the strange new idea filtered slowly into their monster brains. They looked like Dad does when Mum points out the car isn't moving because the handbrake is still on.

**'What an intriguing idea!'** the doctor said. 'And I suppose we don't have anything to lose at this stage. **Well done,** Ozzy. Monster medicine needs more **outside-the-box thinking** like that. I'll make a note of it.' She pulled out a small pink notebook and began to scribble: *less reliance on*

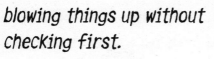

*blowing things up without checking first.*

But since it was my intriguing idea, I was the one who was **'volunteered'** to turn the doorknob.

I peered carefully inside.

There was no sign of Trevor.

But – to my complete surprise – **Inspector Pincher was still alive!** He was curled up on the floor with his claws wrapped tightly round his head. He looked like a **woodlouse.**

'What on earth happened here, Pincher?' asked the doctor as she pressed in behind me. But the inspector wasn't capable of speaking clearly.

'S . . . s . . . s . . . s . . . s . . . s . . . !' was all he managed to stutter. 'S . . . s . . . s . . . sa . . . sa . . . save . . . me!'

**'Never mind him!'** said Delores sympathetically as she barged in past the doctor. She stood looking around the room with a confused expression on her face. (This is exactly like her usual annoyed expression, but the left eyebrow **wobbles** ever so slightly.) 'Where's Trevor the triffid gone?' she demanded. And at the mere mention of the word **'triffid'** the inspector waved one shaky claw towards Delores's desk.

But it wasn't the triffid he was pointing at.

*It was the cutie!*

# REVOLTING!

## Chapter 14

The little creature was just sitting there on Delores's desk, idly chewing one end of a pencil. It looked **exactly** like when I'd first picked it up back in the **FANG-TASTIQUE FUN** shop (i.e. about as cute as a moth-eaten teddy bear).

Definitely not the **dormouse-wearing-dormouse-patterned-pyjamas** level of cute that had given me the **M.U.S.H.** attack.

Even so, I was amazed to see the doctor and Delores staring at it without any anti-Q-T protection. 'Quite extraordinary!' the doctor observed. 'At this distance from a cutie my eyeballs should be as runny as a **troll-cheese fondue.** But look, Ozzy!' She held up a hand. All its six fingers were intact. 'Look! No effect at all!'

'What does it mean?' I asked. But, before she could answer, Sergeant Hairiet peered nervously round the door. Her sudden appearance seemed to alarm the cutie. It *squeaked,* dropped the half-chewed pencil and instantly began to transform. Its eyes stretched open **impossibly wide.** The nose deflated until it was a tiny little button. Even the fur seemed to **puff up** as if had recently been blow-dried at an expensive hair salon.

*The cutie was getting cuter. Right in front of our eyes!*

The doctor's Q-T detector began to buzz angrily and she stared open-mouthed at the reading. **'GOOD GRIEF!'** she cried. **'It's hitting plus six!**

**HAMSTER EATING A SLICE OF BANANA!** And I think it's going to go **FULL CUTIE!'**

'EVERY MONSTER FOR THEMSELVES!' Delores cried, and dived beneath her desk. Sergeant Hairiet *scrabbled* frantically out of the room. The doctor flung one hand up to stop her **eyeballs melting** while the other reached out to where Pincher lay **curled up** on the floor like a frightened supply teacher.

**'Ozzy! Help me move the inspector!'** her muffled voice ordered. 'He won't survive Q-T levels this high – **AAARGHH!'** She backed away, wincing in pain. 'It's no good,' she said. 'You'll have to save him yourself.' And with that she **elbowed** Delores to make some room under the desk.

Now, I would have loved to help. But at that exact moment I was *hopelessly distracted* by the cutie. You see, it was looking about as *adorable* as a *baby otter washing its whiskers*. And all I wanted to do was reach out and stroke the *soft, soft lovely fur* on the top of its gorgeous little –

**OW!** Something hard smacked me in the face.

It was one of the doctor's shoes.

'Snap out of it, Nurse!' she ordered. 'You're in the grip of a full-blown **M.U.S.H.** attack again. Think of something unpleasant. **Something truly and utterly revolting.**'

'**Hang on!**' Delores added. 'I've got a picture of my husband somewhere in my handbag. That should do the trick.'

But it was no good. Any **horrendous** picture of Delores's husband would come far **too late** for the inspector. And possibly for me as well. My hand was already petting the cutie. If I didn't help myself, Pincher would be doomed and I'd be stuck in this **M.U.S.H.** forever. In a **desperate** attempt to push the **M.U.S.H.** out, I tried to recall the most un-cute things that I could. A horrid series of images and smells flashed through my brain.

They were – in order of increasing horribleness:

**1.** The smell of **goblin B.O.**

**2.** Pulling a large sticking plaster off **Wolfgang Werewolf's extremely hairy bottom.**

**3.** Scraping **foot cheese** out from between a **troll's toes.**

*It was working!* With every horrible thing I recalled, I could feel the soppy hypnosis fading to a more manageable level of affection.

I needed one last push, though. So I dredged up the most **revolting** thing I could from my memory – that time I helped change my little sister's nappy. **Ugh!** The dreadful image of it was seared into my mind.

*But it worked!* A moment later, I was myself again.

'Cutie,' I said calmly, 'there's no need to be scared. You can stop that now!' The creature seemed to **instinctively** realize that I meant it no harm and the cuteness began to fade. Its mouth widened, the angelic eyes narrowed and became distinctly shifty. Even the lurid pinky-blue fur 'rippled' into a dull, sludgy colour. The incessant noise of the Q-T detector faded.

**'Incredible!'** exclaimed the doctor. She had emerged from beneath the desk and was now staring with wonder at the cutie. **'Remarkable!** Why, it almost looks **monstrous** now! Well done, Ozzy. I'm deeply impressed by your **steely self-control** in the face of such attractiveness.'

My disobedient hand was still stroking the cutie's soft fur, though. And, interestingly, the creature was responding with a funny little **COOOOOOOOing!** noise. It was enjoying my touch! And as its eyes closed in *blissful* relaxation the most remarkable thing happened. The nose grew more **bulbous,** a pair of tiny horns poked up unexpectedly through the fur and the creature began to smile.

It was a great big **W–I–D–E** smile that was
suddenly filled with a surprisingly large number
of white – and very **pointy** – teeth. It was a
smile that continued to grow. **Wider and
wider and WIDER!** Eventually there
were enough teeth on display to make a **great
white shark** rush to the dentist to demand a
brand-new set of pearly whites.

But these teeth were stained a very familiar
sappy-green colour.

'By my grandmother's formidable
undergarments!' cried the doctor. 'I think
we've just discovered what happened to Trevor.'

'Are you trying to tell me this little ball of

*fluff* ate my husband's homicidal triffid?' asked Delores. She had finally emerged from beneath her desk. She sounded strangely pleased at the unexpected news.

Just then, Inspector Pincher finally spoke. **'It s-s-saved me!'** he stammered. 'Just as the **ghastly** twiffid was about to eat me, that –' he pointed at the cutie – 'that ball of fluff **burst** out of its box and ate every last bit of it. I don't think it was twying to help me. I just think it was **wather hungwy!'** He shuddered at the memory and then finally pushed himself up from the floor. 'Will somebody **please** explain what on earth is going on?'

'Inspector! You're **ALIVE?'** cried Sergeant Hairiet from the doorway. She peered nervously round the corner, wearing a thick pair of **anti-Q-T goggles.**

She also had several floral tea towels from the kitchen wrapped around her head. 'Is it safe to enter?'

'Remarkably, yes,' answered the doctor. She pointed her Q-T meter at the cutie. The needle was now reading a safe and steady -2 **(BIT WEIRD).** Sergeant Hairiet stared from the reading to the cutie and back again in disbelief.

'I don't understand this,' she admitted.

'Isn't it obvious?' said the doctor, smiling a knowing (and, to be honest, slightly **smug)** smile. 'The toxic radiation of cuteness is simply an **evolved defence mechanism.** Cutie's only use their toxic attractiveness when threatened.'

'But how can something be **dangerously** cute one moment, then *charmingly* **monstrous** the next?' Pincher asked. 'It goes against nature!'

'Pincher!' said the doctor. 'Have you forgotten what Professor Twinky used to teach us back in **Monster Ethics 101** at university?'

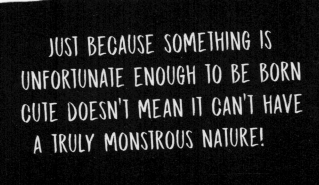

JUST BECAUSE SOMETHING IS UNFORTUNATE ENOUGH TO BE BORN CUTE DOESN'T MEAN IT CAN'T HAVE A TRULY MONSTROUS NATURE!

'I can vouch for that,' I agreed, thinking about my little sister's mealtime habits.

But Inspector Pincher still looked shocked. His world view had clearly been shaken. 'So you're saying my mandibles have been wrong about Q-Ts all these years?' he asked. 'Quite, quite wrong?'

A shiver of embarrassment passed through his mandibles at this admission.

'Not completely,' admitted the doctor. 'Cuties can still be **extremely dangerous** when they choose to be. But if we monsters weren't so completely **terrified** by the very idea of cuteness we might have tried to understand them. Although,' she added, 'it doesn't help when Ozzy's species insists on making artificial ones like in *I WUV U MR SNUGGLE-WUGGLE!*' All the monsters turned to glower at me until the doctor continued. 'But perhaps we could all try to have a more **open mind** about the real cuties in future. Who knows? They may turn out to be as useful as our **disturbingly** *attractive little friend* here.'

'Useful?' snorted Pincher.

'Well, it'll be jolly useful if anyone needs saving from another **homicidal triffid incident,**' she said pointedly.

The inspector's mandibles were still busy arguing amongst themselves. And for a moment I thought he might actually be about to apologize. But then he clacked his claws and barked, **'MANDIBLES! STAND TO ATTENTION!'** and

his floppy mouthparts ceased their bickering and stiffened. He turned angrily on Sergeant Hairiet. 'Sergeant! **Stop gawping** at that furball! Pull yourself together and gather up my equipment! We are leaving.'

The hassled sergeant picked up Pincher's discarded **Von-Punsch gun** and Q-T meter as he addressed the monster doctor.

'You had a lucky escape this time, Dr Sichertall,' he said. 'But just because *this* particular cweature is not dangerous –'

I noticed how he stressed the word 'this' – 'does not mean the monster world is safe. There are still **dangerously** *cute things out there,*' he said ominously. 'Our paths will no doubt cross again.' And with that he **scuttled** from the surgery, several of his mandibles making **rude gestures** at us over his shoulder.

Sergeant Hairiet lingered until her boss was out of earshot and then whispered, 'Thank you for coming to Cringetown.' Then she **winked** that large eye once and followed Pincher out of the surgery.

## So she had been the anonymous caller!

'Well, well, well!' said the doctor, vigorously rubbing her hands together as we all emerged from the booth. 'I must say, Ozzy, this is an amazing development! Professor Twinky is going to be **thrilled to bits** when he arrives to take the cutie away.'

'What?' I said. 'What do you mean, take the cutie away?'

'Why, this is a **major discovery** for the monster community, Ozzy!' said the doctor. 'If we want a world where cuties and monsters can sit peacefully together around a campfire, eating **marsh-mellows** and singing out-of-tune *folk songs*, Professor Twinky's team will have to subject our cutie to an intense research programme for the next **twenty or thirty years.** There will be tests to run, and all manner of probes to be inserted—'

I looked over to where the cutie was – *adorably* – pretending to use the office phone (upside down). 'NO!' I snapped. Then I picked the creature up, hugged it tightly to my chest and backed slowly away from the monster doctor.

# I'M NOT AFRAID OF THAT AT ALL

## Chapter 15

'**N**urse Ozzy!' snapped the doctor. 'Give the little monster to me. You are having another **M.U.S.H.** attack!' She bent to remove her other shoe. Delores settled down on a nearby chair to make sure she had an unobstructed view of the action.

'Possibly,' I admitted. 'But I **won't let you** send him away to be experimented on! Can't we do the research here?'

The doctor made a sneaky grab for the cutie, but missed. I backed away. She lunged again, crying, **'Give it HERE!'** But this sudden movement seemed to frighten the cutie and it began to defensively transform again. It only managed to become as cute as a cheap greetings card, but it was more than the doctor and Delores could bear.

'**AArghughhhh!**' they cried in unison, backing away while trying not to be sick.

'**STOP!**' the doctor shouted. 'All right! All right, Ozzy! Get it to stop doing THAT and I'll tell Professor Twinky not to come.'

I **tickled** the creature gently behind the ears and said, 'Who's a nasty little cutie, then?' and it **instantly** calmed down. Its face grew more **ugly** by the second.

The doctor looked on, amazed.

'Nurse Ozzy!' she said. '**A cutie** *whisperer!* All right. You win. The creature can stay – but it can't **possibly** live here at the surgery.'

'Why not?' I asked, clearly disappointed.

'Well, for one thing,' explained the doctor, 'it might forget itself and have a little . . . **accident.**'

'I'm sure it's toilet-trained,' I said.

'No. I meant it might go all Q-T on us,' explained the doctor. 'Some of my patients only have **three or four weak hearts.** And you may not be aware that accidentally **scaring** patients to death is frowned on by the *Royal College of Monster Doctors.*'

'I'll take him,' interrupted Delores. She had been listening all this time.

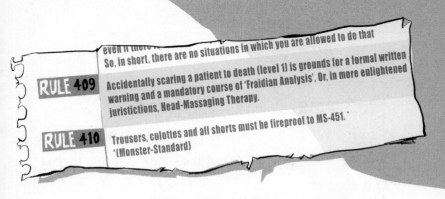

**RULE 409**   Accidentally scaring a patient to death (level 1) is grounds for a formal written warning and a mandatory course of 'Fraidian Analysis'. Or, in more enlightened juristictions, Head-Massaging Therapy.

**RULE 410**   Trousers, culottes and all shorts must be fireproof to MS-451.*
'(Monster-Standard)

'But your husband collects man-eating plants and triffids,' I said.

**'So?'**

'Well, aren't you afraid that the cutie will eat them all?' I asked.

**'Oh no,'** said Delores, as innocently as was possible with her **monstrous** features (i.e. not very much). 'I'm not afraid of that at all!' She picked the cutie up with one tentacle while another two began to **tickle** it behind the horns.

'But what if it gets scared and turns all cute?' I asked.

'It'll be worth it just to keep my husband's **horrible plants** under control,' Delores said. 'Come on, you **revolting** little object. We're going home. And I hope you've still got your appetite.'

**'Heavens, Ozzy,'** said the doctor as Delores

left. 'What a first few weeks you've had. First helping Bob the Blob find a use for his **snot**. And now our **MOMENTOUS** discovery that cuties aren't as dangerous as most monsters believe **AND** that they are the natural predators of triffids! **My word!** It took me a hundred and eighty-five years before my first official submission to OGBERT & NISH!' A faraway look crossed her face. 'It was called

"Troll earwax – a revolutionary application for parasitic nasal worms".'

'You discovered a cure for nasal worms?' I said.

'Of course not.' She laughed. 'Why on earth would anyone want to **cure** nasal worms? You strange creature! **No, no, no.** Troll wax encourages them!'

She opened a drawer in Delores's desk and pulled out headed notepaper and a pen. She **plonked** it down in front of me. 'Pull up a chair,' she said. 'We have a paper to write for submission to Mr Ogbert and Madame Nish immediately.'

THE END

# CODA:

Extract from Ogbert & Nish's *Bumper Book of Monster Maladies*, edition no. 43563456543(b)

## TRIFFIDS

### TREATMENT FOR HOMICIDAL RAGE (UPDATE):

Until recently there was no cure apart from precise application of small nuclear weapons. This treatment– despite being successful – had unpleasant side-effects. However, recent events have revealed that triffids DO have at least one natural predator. This monster is known as 'the cutie'. It is as effective as an atomic bomb, but a great deal easier to clean up after.

EDITOR'S NOTE: If you have a homicidal triffid problem, then please get in touch with:

Annie von Sichertall VIII M.D.D. F.R.S.C.D.
(and Nurse Ozzy Ordinary)
At 10 Lovecraft Avenue,
Screechdale,
MON 5TR

# My Diary – A Cutie

Dear Diary,

Today was fun!

I popped out this morning for something to eat. But my favourite snack bar was closed. How inconsiderate! I tried to get in another way, but got so tired I had to have a little lie-down.

I was having the loveliest dream about rampaging giant triffids when I was woken up by a weird-looking monster. I was a bit annoyed at first, but they gave me ever such a nice cuddle that I forgave them. Anyway, it turned out they'd made me a lovely comfy box to sleep in. So I got in and had a super cosy snooze in there until I was woken up again by the smell of

my favourite food. I let myself out and
was amazed to find that the weird-
looking monster had put out a lovely
juicy triffid for me to eat.

How thoughtful of them!

Anyway, I was so hungry I ate the
WHOLE thing.

Then, just as I was about to have
another snooze, a nice, happy-looking lady
came along and gave me a lovely cuddle.
Then she popped me in her comfy bag
and took me home.

Her house is ever so lovely! And she's
got all kinds of delicious things to eat
here. It's like living in a buffet.

She's EVER so friendly. I think I might
stay for a bit.

Anyway, it's time for bed now.

Night-night!

# APPENDIX:

## I WUV U MR SNUGGLE-WUGGLE

Much has been written in the monster world about the human phenomena I WUV U MR SNUGGLE-WUGGLE but since most of it is quite rude we can't print any of it here. Suffice to say, most monsters and things consider I WUV U MR SNUGGLE-WUGGLE the wickedest thing ever done by human beings.

Most of its characters register an incredibly dangerous +6 on the Potter-Poe scale, with Mr Snuggle-Wuggle himself hitting +7 on at least nine of the pages in book one. (The illustration on page thirteen is potentially lethal.)

The book's 'cunning' combination of toxic cuteness and subtle brainwashing seems to have ensnared the entire human population. Since publication, the book and its sequels (*I STIW WUV U MR SNUGGLE-WUGGLE* and *PLEASE COME HOME MR SNUGGLE-WUGGLE*) have sold over

630 million copies worldwide. It has also spawned seven equally appalling films.

There has been an award-winning TV series, countless loved toys, lunchboxes, toothbrushes, underwear, hats and (obviously) an annoyingly smart range of expensive furniture.

In short, this makes it almost impossible for innocent monsters who are stumbling, creeping or lurching around the human world, minding their own business, to avoid dangerous contamination.

As a consequence the author-illustrator, Tarquin Cleever, has been declared a criminal by the all-dimensions Monster Council. A reward of 100 million Karloffz has been offered for his capture alive (but preferably dead).

# GLOSSARY

**Backhand:** A technique that uses an offensive weapon (e.g. an axe, tennis racket or shower towel) in an overly showy manner.

**Boy band:** Boy bands appeared from nowhere and spread like wildfire through the human world for two decades. Their cute faces and disgustingly sweet music are lethal to any exposed monster.

**Cacophony:** A painfully loud out-of-tune chorus. Famous examples include: the detonation of a triffid seed-bomb and a human classroom three seconds before the teacher enters.

**Dancing:** A much loved art in the monster community. Modern styles range from the earth-shattering intensity of Tokyo's Kaiju Monster ballet company, to the intricate cape-stylings of Vampire Flamenco.

**Dragon:** Despite the armour-plated scales of their exterior, their razor-sharp teeth and tendency to act like an unpredictable flying flame-thrower, most dragons aren't actually that dangerous. As long as you remember three simple rules:

1. Do not wave a sword in their face.
2. Do not carry around large amounts of gold.
3. Never EVER climb down a dragon's throat.

**Folk song:** Along with the Jammy Dodger, folk music is one of the few human creations that is still extremely popular with monsters. There is something wonderfully comforting about the strange hairy creatures that produce the music, and the harsh warbling sound is reminiscent of the lullabies sung by monster mothers to their children at bedtime.

**Fondue:** A human food that achieved brief popularity in the monster world on account of its naked flame, boiling hot liquid cheese and sharpened steel needles. It was eventually banned after a series of dinner parties turned into small regional wars.

DAILY SPIKE
FIGHT BREAKS OUT AT FONDUE WAR PEACE DINNER

**Grandma:** Grandmas are the only known entity in the universe (apart from the notorious Q-Ts) that can switch at will between the two poles of the Potter-Poe scale.

**Infra-purple:** This colour lies between Radioactive red and Bleeding-eyes blue. Its extreme garishness and tendency to induce migraines make it a popular choice for the lights on emergency vehicles, as well as with painters who dislike critics.

**Gross-flatulator:** Nobody enjoys the expulsion of excess gas as much as a healthy, green blooded monster. But there has to be some kind of a limit. Gross-flatulators disagree.

**Karaoke:** A highly skilled form of human torture. The victim is forced to maintain a smile whilst listening to a friend or family member butcher their favourite song.

**Mammoth racing:** A monster sport that used a thrilling combination of thunderous galloping and extreme hairstyling. It was unfortunately disbanded in the year 1650 BC, after the infamous Wrangell Island pile-up caused the total extinction of the mammoth species.

**Miggimuss:** One of the most infamous cuties created by humanity. It is impossible for the writer to even attempt to describe due to the risk of involuntary vomiting.

**Mime:** The art of communicating pointless ideas without the aid of words. Famous examples include: 'I'm trapped behind this glass screen', 'I'm pulling on a rope for some reason' and 'Help! Help! I'm being eaten by the audience'.

**Poo bag:** Specialised equipment used in the popular human sport of poo-catching. The sport involves a human following a small furry animal around and picking up its droppings. Alas, the scoring system is completely baffling to monsters.

**Reality TV:** A cunning scheme devised by monsters to find and identify humans who should be avoided at all costs.

**Snake-grooming parlours:** Snake grooming parlours turn the tedious chore of skin shedding into a pleasurable morning out. At the salon, you drop off your old skin and subsequently lounge about swallowing baby chicks as the stylists primp and preen your fresh new scales.

**Sunburn:** Human beings lack the necessary scales, crusty skin or slimy gloop to adequately protect themselves from nuclear radiation. Despite this, they insist on lying motionless in their underpants beneath the largest atomic bomb in the solar system. They call the radioactive scorching 'Sunburn'.

**Tendril:** A pale vegetable imitation of a tentacle.

**Zombie-weasels:** Ordinary weasels make charming pets for monsters due to their razor-sharp teeth and delightfully wriggly bodies, which move like fur covered tentacles. However, excessive petting can cause malfunctions. To combat this flaw, Dr Guddidea Athetime attempted to genetically engineer a sturdier weasel, but unfortunately his test subjects escaped from the lab and became the impossible to kill pest that we know and hate today.

Turn the page to read an exclusive extract from Ozzy and the doctor's next howlingly hilarious adventure, **Monster Doctor: Slime Crime**

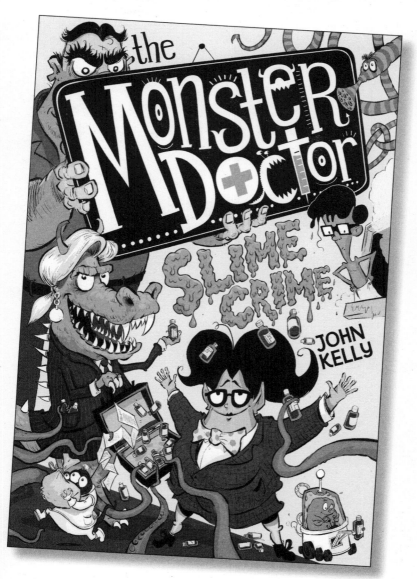

# 'IS IT A LEAFY GREEN?'

## Chapter 1

The monster doctor's voice crackled from the heavy walkie-talkie dangling on my belt.

*'What is the precise colour of the boil, nurse Ozzy? Over!'*

I didn't reply, because at that very moment both of my hands were **terribly** busy preventing me from falling off the top of a **hundred foot tall ladder**. To distract myself from the dreadful drop below, I looked closer at the huge boil that was six inches from my face.

It was about the size of an **over-inflated space hopper** and looked very angry indeed.

The boil was attached to the end of an enormous nose, and that nose was attached to an equally enormous giant called **Little Lionel.** (Lionel is small for a giant. Hence his name. Most giants are about two hundred feet tall. So Lionel's probably just a borderline ogre, to be honest.)

*'Come in nurse Ozzy!'* said the doctor's insistent voice. *'I repeat: what colour is—'*

'I CAN'T REACH THE RADIO!' I bellowed down towards where the doctor stood holding the foot of the **wobbly** ladder. The animated blob of messy hair, tweed and industrial framed glasses that is Annie Von Sichertall – a.k.a. the monster doctor, a.k.a. my boss – looked up at me. And, not for the first time, I wondered why it was me perched dangerously on top of this ridiculously tall ladder examining an **ogre's boil** instead of the monster doctor herself.

When we had arrived a few minutes earlier and extended the ladder from the roof of Lance the ambulance, I had asked her, 'Why don't you climb up there?'

The monster doctor's answer had seemed very convincing at the time. But now, in hindsight, I couldn't remember what it was. It was something about her **dodgy left knee** or an insurance policy having lapsed. I forget which.

*'Nurse Ozzy!'* her voice gently chided me from the radio. *'A monster doctor never shouts in front of*

*a patient – unless they insist on lecturing you about a*
*silly treatment they've found on the monsterweb. Then*
*you can really let rip at—'*

'THE BOIL IS BRIGHT GREEN!' I shouted in
order to cut off her rambling.

*'Ah! Now that's rather interesting,' she said.*
*'Would you say it was a leafy green? Or closer to the*
*lovely green of freshly exuded troll pus?'*

I thought about that for a moment. After three
weeks as the monster doctor's assistant, I was
now well acquainted with all the wondrous shades
of troll pus.

'NEITHER,' I replied. 'IT'S MORE LIKE THE
CHUNKY BITS IN DELORES' PISTACHIO AND
PHLEGM BISCUITS.'

Delores is our surgery's
grumpy receptionist.
I can't decide which
is scarier: Delores
or the contents of her
special biscuit tin.

Delores' biscuits

Somewhere down below I felt Lionel's mouth
begin to open. Oh no! He was going to speak
again. I grabbed on tight to the ladder's rungs.

# 'SPOT... NOT... THERE... AT... BREAKFAST!'

he said in a voice as slow and loud as a passing car stereo. (Giants aren't stupid by the way. The reason they speak like that is on account of their brains being so **MASSIVE** that it takes an age for information to travel from point A to point B. About as slowly as Mum and Dad learning how a new TV works.)

*'EXTRAORDINARY!'* exclaimed the doctor. *'So this boil is almost as fast-growing as a human teenager's acne!'*

Then she went silent for a moment.

This was worrying.

When the monster doctor goes quiet it means one of three things:

**1.** She has run away.

**2.** She is stuck in the pharmacy cupboard again. (We really should get that door fixed.)

**3.** She's about to ask me to do something **very dangerous** and is thinking of a nice way to put it.

'*Ozzy,*' she continued in a suspiciously innocent voice, '*I wonder if you could just give the boil a gentle tap and measure how much it wobbles.*'

'I'VE ALREADY DONE THAT,' I shouted smugly. I had just read the **MONSTER MALADIES** chapter on **DIAGNOSTIC JELLIFICATION** (The D-J scale\*) the previous night. *MONSTER MALADIES* is a wonderful book about the most common monster illnesses out there, and it has a lot of really useful stuff every trainee monster doctor needs to know. There's a good section about running very fast.

'**IT'S NOT VERY WOBBLY!**' I shouted. '**I'D RATE IT ABOUT 4.5 DJs.**' This was about as jellylike as a mostly-inflated football.

---

\* FYI the D-J scale runs from 0.0 (granite and dried-on baby food) to 10.0 (fresh dog drool).

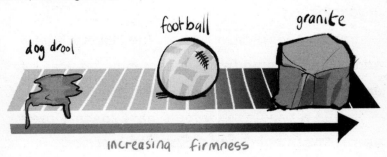

dog drool

football

granite

increasing firmness

## Bob the Blob

'*That's not right,*' mused the doctor through the radio. '*A boil that size should have a squishy consistency somewhere between Bob the Blob and human brains or blancmange. You'd better take a sample, nurse Ozzy. There's a medium monster needle in your kit.*'

I shifted very carefully on the rickety ladder and rooted around in the emergency medical kit dangling from my right shoulder. My fingers closed on a needle that would have made a pretty useful **spear point for a Spartan warrior.**

'*I'm very sorry*,' I said, holding the huge syringe up in front of Lionel's giant crossed eyes. 'But I need to use this.'

Fortunately monsters aren't as squeamish about needles as humans are.

'NO. . . PROBLEM. . .' he boomed. 'ONLY . . . A. . . TEENY. . . WEENY . . . LITTLE . . . NEEDLE.'

He laughed gently, almost knocking me off the ladder. But I held on grimly until the ladder — and my teeth — stopped rattling.

'*Remember, Ozzy!*' the doctor reminded me. '*Giants are as thick-skinned as a TV talent show candidate. You'll have to give it* **a bit of welly.**'

I gripped the syringe, took a deep breath and swung it down with as much force as I could, as if I were trying to cut a piece of *my Gran's pastry*. As the sharp point punctured the tough skin of the boil, there was a noise that reminded me of mealtimes at home.

It was a louder version of the noise my **baby sister** makes when she suddenly decides that the food she has been chewing would be better back on the plate. Or the nearby wall. Or my face.

It was a

# SPLAT!

But much, much, louder.

And all of a sudden I was very wet and the same colour as the chunky bits in one of Delores' pistachio and phlegm biscuits.

## TO BE CONTINUED ...

# ACKNOWLEDGEMENTS

I'd like to thank the following people
for the chance to write another one
of these ridiculous books.

My wife Cathy, who manages to effortlessly
move between +3 and -3 on the Poe-Potter scale.
My agents Jodie, Emily and Molly at United
Agents, who are always talking sense when I'm
not. Everyone at Macmillan for continuing to
believe in the Monster Doctor; but especially Cate,
Lucy, Sue and Amanda who together somehow
manage to make it look as though I actually
know what I'm doing.

## DISCLAIMER

*Any reader suffering from lingering **M.U.S.H.** hypnosis can treat themselves at home by simply Googling something monstrous. I would recommend close-ups of a spider's face or photographs of men's hair styles from the 1970s.*

# ABOUT THE AUTHOR

John Kelly is the author and
illustrator of picture books such as
*The Beastly Pirates* and *Fixer*, the
author of picture books *Can I Join
Your Club* and *Hibernation Hotel*, and
the illustrator of fiction series such
as *Ivy Pocket* and *Araminta Spook*.
He has twice been shortlisted for the
Kate Greenaway prize, with *Scoop!*
and *Guess Who's Coming for Dinner*.
The Monster Doctor series is his first
author-illustrator middle-grade fiction.